MW01675906

THE LEGEND OF ANNIE CROW

MICHAEL W. MOUNTAIN

Copyright © 2021 by MICHAEL W. MOUNTAIN.

All rights reserved. No part of this publication may be reproduced, distributed, or transmitted in any form or by any means, including photocopying, recording, or other electronic or mechanical methods, without the prior written permission of the author, except in the case of brief quotations embodied in critical reviews and certain other noncommercial uses permitted by copyright law.

This book is a complete work of fiction. Any references to historical events, real people, or real locales are used fictitiously. Other names, characters, places and incidents are a product of the author's imagination, and any resemblance to actual events or locales or persons, living or dead, is entirely coincidental.

Printed in the United States of America.

Library of Congress Control Number: 2021907371

ISBN	Paperback	978-1-64803-627-9
	eBook	978-1-64803-628-6

Westwood Books Publishing LLC
11416 SW Aventino Drive
Port Saint Lucie, FL 34987

www.westwoodbookspublishing.com

DEDICATION

In memory of Gerald Hollingworth Rudsdil,
my dear friend and cousin.

In memory of my Aunt June Genevieve Rudsdil, my second mother.

May they both rest in peace.

CONTENTS

CHAPTER ONE

FAMILY

My name is now Annie Crow, but I'll expound on that later. However, my given name was Annie O'Grady, and my folks were from the far away country called Ireland. My daddy's name was Patrick and my mommy's name was Kathleen. I also had three brothers: Jimmy, Pete and Billy. My entire family was murdered by a band of Cheyenne Indians in 1865, when I think I was around ten years old. Our wagon was attacked, and everyone was killed except me. Again, I'll get back to all of that a little later.

Daddy wanted us all to move west with him so he could pan for gold. I should explain to you that my daddy was a very lazy man. At least that's what Mommy used to tell us. Back in the north where we were from, we all lived and worked on a very unproductive farm. The owner of the property, Mr. James, forced us to leave because Daddy refused to work hard enough. Mr. James stated emphatically, "The reason I'm evicting you folks from my land is that all my sharecroppers have produced except for you O'Grady's! You Mr. O'Grady, are the most worthless farmer I've ever seen, and I've seen many. I'm so sorry about this Mrs. O'Grady, but as you know, I have warned your worthless husband too many times about his lackadaisical work ethic. I will find a place for you and your children to live, as long as this slovenly man you call your husband is nowhere around. If I were to find out he's still in your lives, well, I'd have to kick you all out too."

Needless to say, Daddy wouldn't allow Mommy and us kids to accept any of the charity Mr. James was offering. He spit in Mr. James face as he was loading a wagon, which Mr. James said was his wagon. It mattered none to my daddy and I remember his exact words, "Screw you James and the horse you rode in on, you dirty son-of-a-bitch, all you want is to bed my wife." I was a bit confused at the time about the 'bed my wife' comment. Did Mr. James want to sleep with Mommy? What harm could that do? Later I figured it out. After we had loaded up our small number of belongings, Daddy screamed again at Mr. James, "I'm coming for you, I'll get you for what you've done to my family. I'll get you!"

Mr. James replied, "I didn't do shit to your family, you did, you worthless piece of shit. Good riddance Mr. O'Grady. I'm happy I finally got you outta of my life and off my property."

I forgot to say that my daddy was also a drunk. And when I say he was a drunk, I mean he was a mean drunk; I mean a really mean drunk! Whenever he could get his hands on some 'shine' as Daddy called it, he'd get so drunk he wouldn't come home for days. Well, after we left our farm, we lived out of that old wagon for a long while. One night Daddy came home drunk and yelled, "We're leaving now, get your asses up and get ready."

Mommy looked at him and said, "Patrick, your clothes are soaked with blood. Whose blood is that?"

Daddy screamed, "It's none of your business, just get ready."

Mommy was angry, she screamed back, "Whose blood is that? Did you try and kill Mr. James?"

Daddy replied back, "I did no such thing. I just helped a friend butcher a pig, that's all. Now let's get going."

Mommy just shook her head and said, "You are a lying bastard, you killed Mr. James. The law will get you, you stupid shit."

Us kids were all awake and were listening to all that was said. My brother Jimmy said, "That old fool killed Mr. James. Mommy would never talk like that had he not killed him. I wonder where we'll end up?"

Mommy finally said, "Just where in the hell are we going?"

"We're going to Montana to pan for gold. I hear from a reliable source that there is gold out there and it's just for the taking. Every creek and stream are loaded with the shit. In just a matter just of a few days and we'll be rich."

Mommy replied, "We'll need supplies such as food, water and warm clothing. Also, a couple more work horses and they aren't cheap. Just where in the hell are you going to get money for all of the necessities?"

Daddy responded, "Don't worry your bitchy little self about the money. I just came into some a few days ago and I got plenty for the trip. Now, get your asses moving, we need to get outta here pronto, did you hear me?"

Mommy wouldn't relent, she said, "I'm not going anywhere until you tell me where you got the money. Did you kill Mr. James and steal some money from him?"

"No! I didn't kill anyone. I won the money in a card game at the saloon in town. I played poker and won all the money. Now, get moving." Mommy knew he'd killed Mr. James and that's how he got the money. We were so poor we couldn't even buy food, let alone have enough money for Daddy to play poker. In my opinion, he didn't help kill a pig and he never worked a lick to accumulate any money. He either stole it or killed for it. Either way we had to leave the area immediately so he wouldn't go to jail. Within an hours' time, we were traveling west as fast as our sorry team could walk. We stopped in the town of Buford to get supplies and Daddy bought two other horses. All of us kids even got new britches, jackets, hats and gloves. Mommy got a new dress and a jacket too. She seemed sort of happy and it had been a long time since we had seen her sort of happy.

The following day we left for the Montana Territory. We had no idea how long it would take but we knew it was a long trip. Daddy told us a bunch of lies that the trip would only take a couple a weeks, but we all knew better. Mommy got over her happiness quickly and she became very quiet. She walked along beside the wagon and never spoke unless one of us kids asked her a question. I never heard her utter a single word to Daddy for the rest of her life, except when we were attacked. She was a broken woman and Daddy was responsible for her demise. I was only about ten years old and I already hated my daddy.

CHAPTER TWO

DEATH ON THE PRAIRIE

We had been traveling for several months now and we were all very weary. We were also very hungry, well not very hungry, but starving. My stupid daddy didn't know how to hunt and he also didn't know what on the prairie was edible. We had run out of water too and we felt the end was very near unless someone found us. Well, they found us. Mommy spotted them first and she cried out loud, "Indians, up on that hill. Patrick, where are the guns, we'll need your guns?"

My dumb-ass daddy proclaimed, "We don't have no guns. I didn't think we'd need them. I don't think we have much to worry about, there are only three Injuns on that hill."

As I told you earlier, I was only around ten at the time, but I thought my daddy was stupid and if I had any doubts before, his comments erased all my doubts. I knew we were now dead meat. I looked up onto that hill again and there were now about ten warriors watching us. Within two minutes they came down that hill screaming and hollering. They had no guns, just bows and arrows.

There really was no battle, just death to my three brothers and my mommy. I didn't care about my daddy, but he was the first to be killed. They scalped him while he was alive, and he was yelling and screaming in pain before they slit his throat. My mommy died with three arrows to her chest. My poor brothers were scalped like Daddy was and then they slit their throats. I sat on the seat of the wagon and watched all the carnage. Not one of those Injuns had looked at me sitting on that wagon seat. I thought they hadn't seen me, but I was so wrong.

After the hooting and the hollering had subsided, their attention was on me. I think I may have been in what is called shock. I showed no emotion, no crying and no tears. But I never really cried that much before, at least that I could remember. I was told I was spoiled by my daddy, but mommy said I wasn't. She said I was just a strong-willed little girl and I now realize that I was physically and mentally strong too.

The Chief Injun walked up to the wagon and grabbed me by my hair and pulled me down to the ground. All the braves were laughing at me. I jumped up and kicked the Chief Injun in the shin. Since I had on boots, I think it might have hurt. He limped a short distance away before returning and he then slapped me hard across the face. I had fallen over onto the ground, but I got up quickly without shedding a tear and stared at him. He tried to put his hand on my face and was uttering somethings I couldn't understand. After I realized his hand was close to my mouth, I bit his hand as hard as I could. He jumped back and was about to slice me open with his knife when another brave stopped him. The brave spoke in a very quiet manner and the Injun I thought was the chief, was now clearly not the chief. He just put his knife in its sheaf and walked to his horse. All the other Injuns were laughing hysterically at the guy that I had bit. The new chief gently reached for my hand and held it in his and walked me towards his horse. He lifted me up and put me in front of him as he mounted the horse. They left my family there to rot in the sun, and they never took one thing from our wagon, just our horses and me. They just wanted us dead. But why didn't they kill me? I soon found out.

CHAPTER THREE

The Tribe

The Cheyenne were fearless warriors and they had a very large presence in Montana. At the time when I was taken, there were over three thousand Cheyenne in the area. That three thousand was divided among about ten to twelve smaller individual tribes. Because of the constant warring between tribes and the fighting with the white settlers, the male population of the Cheyenne tribes was getting depleted. The women dominated the individual tribes and owned most of the tepees and livestock. When a brave died, his brother would marry the widow and take on the responsibility for the children. If there were no brothers, another brave could marry the widow if she were still in her childbearing days. The unmarried widows were women that had passed the age of reproducing or were unable to reproduce because of other issues. If a widow was not wanted because she was too old or couldn't reproduce, she would care for herself.

When I arrived in this Cheyenne camp, I was given to a squaw that couldn't reproduce. The chief carried out a long conversation with her, but I couldn't understand a word he was saying. My guess was he was telling her I was a bit of trouble and be careful not to turn her back on me. I thought that was good advice. I promised myself I wouldn't let her push me around. I was supposed to be a slave to this old bitch until

I could be married, well not necessarily married, but able to reproduce. Little did this old bitch know I was tough as nails.

The squaw's name, which I found out much later, was Pe'ee'ese, or in the English language Big Nose. She had the biggest nose I'd ever seen, and I could see why none of the braves wanted to bed her. She was also mean and a very crabby old lady. After her conversation with the Chief, she came over to me and grabbed me by my hair and pulled me along to a wooded area just outside the camp. She pulled up her deerskin dress and leaned against the tree and peed. She then motioned to me to do the same. As I was squatting down to pee, I realized my brand-new dress was torn and was soaked with mud and dirt. This must have happened when these Injuns were dragging me around.

After our get together pee, she grabbed my hair again and began to drag me back into the compound. I reached down to the ground while I was being dragged and picked up a good-sized rock. I hid it behind my back and waited for her to stop. When we got back to her tepee, she let me stand, which was the dumbest thing she could have done. After I was on both of my feet, I hauled off and hit her directly in her big nose with my rock. Her head dropped into her hands and I slugged her again, this time on the top of her head. She staggered and dropped to her knees. I hit her again, this time on the back of her head. That was the last thing I remembered.

I woke up with my hands tied in front of me and a noose around my neck with the rest of the rope attached to a pole. The chief was standing in front of me with six other braves. My guess is that they were wondering what to do with me. Since I was only ten years old, I thought they didn't want to kill me. But I thought I'd better change my attitude for a while. After staring at me for a few minutes they just walked away.

It wasn't until that night I realized what they were going to do to me. They were going to leave me out in the cold and exposed to all the bugs and animals that would attempt to feast on my little body. I was starving, cold and all alone. It was then it hit me that I had lost all of my family. I didn't care too much that I lost Daddy, he was not a good daddy. He was a drunk and was lazy and he cared for only himself. But losing Mommy and my brothers made me finally cry. Mommy was so good to me as were my brothers. I know I was spoiled by all of them and I missed that. But they all loved me, and I loved them. What was I going to do now? I promised myself I'd be strong, and I wouldn't give in and I wouldn't let any of these Injuns take advantage of me. I'm young and small but I'm not afraid of any of them. They had better never leave me alone or leave me with a weapon. If they did, they'd be sorry.

CHAPTER FOUR

BREAKING ANNIE

I was tied to that pole for two days with no food or water. I knew I was dying. The mosquito's, flies and other insects were feasting on my little body. The dogs in the camp were sniffing and growling at me and my guess was they were ready to have me for dinner. As I was looking into the eyes of a snarling very large dog, I heard a whack and a whimper. It was Big Nose and she had just hit that dog with a large branch. All the dogs ran away, and Big Nose set a piece of buffalo jerky in front of me and a cup of water. I looked her over and her nose was bigger than it had been, and she had a big bump on her forehead. She had a look of disgust on her face and she rattled off something I didn't understand. I replied to her drivel, "You better be careful old lady, I'll get you again."

After I uttered my response a voice said, "Little girl, you'd better be careful, if you don't, you'll be used as bear bait."

Both Big Nose and I looked up and there was an older woman in full Indian garb smiling at me. I asked, "So, you speak English. Are you an Injun?"

The woman was very pretty and didn't have the darker complexion as Big Nose had. She said, "Yes, I know English and I also know Cheyenne and French, I'm what you call fluent in all those languages. Are you in much pain?"

I said, "I hurt all over, but I'll never cry or show them I'm in pain. I'll never give up. Who are you and why are you here?"

The lady smiled and said, "I respect your courage but if you want to live, you'll have to change your attitude. If you don't, they will kill you. You saw what they did to your family, didn't you? They won't hesitate to do the same to you. You are alive only because you are a young girl. They need women here to reproduce, that means having babies. You do know that women have the babies, don't you? Did your mother tell you anything about that sort of thing?"

I was confused and said, "Mommy didn't talk about having babies to me or to my brothers. She did tell me once that Daddy chased her around all the time at night and she hated. I don't know what she hated about that."

The woman kept smiling and said, "Oh sweetie, you are so young. Listen, I'll be around to see you after you're finished with this torture. Keep quiet and do as your told. And do as the Nose here tells you to do."

"Is her name Nose?"

"In English her given name is Big Nose. The Indians here in this tribe do not understand English, so if you call her Nose, no one will understand. Be good and I'll sneak you some more food later tonight."

After she and the Nose had walked away, I thought, *'Just maybe I have found a friend. Or maybe she just trying to get me to give in. What will I do? I have to eat, and I also know I can't take much more of this pain. Like I use to say to Mommy, I promise I'll be good, but I never was. Oh boy, do I miss Mommy and my brothers."* I started to cry. I cried very hard until I fell asleep. When I woke, the compound was very busy with everyone doing their daily chores. The Nose came by and left me a cup of water. I said to her as she was leaving, "Thanks Nose, you bitch."

She stopped and came back with a smile on her face. She muttered something and nodded her head up and down like she had just accomplished something. Well, she didn't. I'd wait until I could get her again.

I remained tied to that pole for five long days. After three days, the food became more plentiful as did the water. My new friend came by late every night and brought me some kind of sweets. They were so good. I never had anything that good in my life. When she showed up, my saliva glands began to work overtime, and my mouth was like a waterfall. When I got the sweets into my mouth, I had a hard time just sucking on them, I wanted to chew them to bits. I realized right away I had to savor the experience and slowly suck on the sweets, but it was so difficult to do. I wondered if my new friend would continue to give me the sweets after I was released for my bondage. I doubted it.

CHAPTER FIVE

NEW HOME

After five days I was released from the post. I still had the rope around my neck, and I was led away by none other than the Nose. She smiled at everyone that we walked by and she talked to them like she had just tamed a wild stallion. She was so smug. After we arrived at her tepee and she grabbed the rope and forced me down on the ground with it. She mumbled some words that I didn't understand and pointed her finger at me. I was confused and before I could open my mouth, she grabbed the rope and tightened it so I couldn't breathe. I began to choke, and my eyes were watering so much I couldn't see. I tried to get up, but she just kicked me back down. I don't remember much, but I do know I must have passed out. When I woke, she was standing over me laughing at me. She then hauled off and kicked me in my side. The rope had left a painful burn mark on my neck and I thought for sure this crazy bitch was going to kill me. So, I did what every ten-year-old girl would do under the same circumstances, I laid on my back and I kicked her as hard as I could with my new boots in her kneecap. A look of pain and surprise covered her face and she fell to the ground. She grabbed her knee screaming and crying. So much for the tough big Nose Indian.

The Nose laid on the ground and cried and couldn't stop. I must have kicked her in a bad place in her knee. Several of the squaws came to her aid. My new friend was one of them and she was not happy. She said, "Get up off the ground and take that rope off your neck, you are coming with me."

I stared at the Nose and laughed while I struggled trying to get the rope off my neck, it was still on very tight. My new friend said, "Let me help you." She reached for a knife in a sheaf that was on her hip and cut the rope.

She said, "Follow me, you little brat."

When she said the brat thing, I knew I was in trouble. We walked a short distance to her tepee and she pulled the cover to the opening away and said, "Get in there."

After I got in the tepee I said, "I'm sorry I kicked her, but she almost killed me. I couldn't breathe. I just lost my temper and I kicked her. Sorry."

She replied, "My Cheyenne name is Manda, which means Harmony. My given name was Sally Albright. I came to this tribe when I was eleven years old. I was spared for the same reason you were spared, to reproduce. In other words, make babies. I made six of them and you met my oldest after they killed your family. He is the Chief here and his name is Avonaco or translated into English, Leaning Bear. Three of my children were killed in battle and my two daughters died in childbirth. I have only Avonaco left. I never married any of the braves, so I don't know who the father of my children were. I was forced into this life and I had no way out, just like you do now. I tried to tell you when you were tied to that post, just give in and do what you're told to do. It's not the best life, but it's better than being dead. And having children is the most wonderful part of this life."

I listened intently to what Manda had said but I couldn't fathom living like her. I was getting the hint about making babies now. I kind of guessed before but I wasn't sure until now. I knew I'd never let a man, white or Indian do that to me without me wanting him to. I'd kill them before it happened.

Manda said, "You've become very quiet, don't you have anything to say?"

I said, "I'm too young to understand all you've said. I think my birthday was a few days ago, so I may be eleven now but I'm not sure. That's not old enough to understand about making babies. But I will tell you one thing right now and I don't expect I'll change my mind; I will not stay here like you did and make babies for these Injuns. They might as well kill me now, because if they don't, I'll kill them all later."

Manda replied, "What is your given name?"

"It's Annie. Annie O'Grady."

"Well Annie O'Grady, you'll be living with me from now on. Please don't try and hurt me, because I don't want to hurt you. Do you understand?"

I replied, "Alright, I understand! But Manda, you'll have to understand, if you're nice to me, I'll be nice to you."

"There are some rules you'll have to adhere to, and I explain all of them in detail. I'll make sure your stay is not painful. But, whatever you do, stay away from the Nose. Do you understand that Annie? If you go near her, she has said it to all that would listen, she'd kill you."

"I'll stay clear of her for now, but when I get older, who knows?"

CHAPTER SIX

ADJUSTING

Manda led me out of her tepee and over to one of her gardens. She said, "You and I will work to keep the varmints out of the gardens and your job will also be to water. The water jugs are here, and you know where the creek is. Our band will be moving when the cold weather begins in the next few months. We'll need food for the winter, and we'll provide some of that. Also, our hunting parties will be on the lookout for the buffalo herds. We'll need at least fifteen or more buffalo for food this winter. We'll also need their fur for clothing and to trade for other supplies. Our braves have accumulated several rifles and ammunition from the settlers but there is a need for more. Rifles will help in our hunting and to defend us from settlers and the army. Any questions?"

I was perplexed and said, "If I understand you right, the tribe wants more guns so they can kill more of us?"

"Yes, for protection and for hunting."

"What do we do when the braves kill a buffalo?"

Manda smiled before saying, "We gut and skin the buffalo and cut up the meat. Our men do the hunting and kill the beasts and we then take over. At first the smell and the blood and guts will be difficult to take but you'll get used to it."

After our little talk and walk, I began to look around the camp. I saw many of the tribe, both men and women talking and teasing one another. The kids were also playing and laughing. I finally looked at the surrounding area and I found it was really a beautiful setting. There were many birch, pine, evergreen, maple, oak and apple trees. I hadn't realized it, but the camp was situated high in the hills. It was almost like a fort. I guess it was a fort. They could see for miles around and if the army or other tribes were going to attack, they'd be able to fend them off. These Cheyenne were smart, very smart.

Manda must have gotten the okay from her son to let me roam around the campsite by myself. She must have told him and the others she had me under control, after all I think I'm eleven years old now and I'll do as she says. Ha! As I roamed the campsite, I could hear all the tribal members whispering as I passed by. I couldn't understand a thing they were saying but I did hear the name Pe'ee'ese being muttered. I'm now sure the Nose is going to try and kill me. I sure hope Manda will protect me. After my slow walk around the camp, I returned to Manda's tepee. She was standing outside with another woman chatting in Cheyenne. Of course, I again didn't understand what they were saying. The other woman said in broken English, "Hel…loo. I Moree'e. My name mea…ns Little Wom…an. I made you some…things.

I looked Moree'e over and she was in fact a little woman and seemed very nice. I smiled back and said, "Who taught you to speak English?"

She replied, "It Man…da. I don't speak we…ll."

Manda said, "She's only been learning the language for a couple of months now, but she does understand what I'm saying when I talk to her now. She's the only tribal member that has ever tired except my grandson Wild Wind. The way I see it, in order to trade with the whites, we'll need to understand them. I'm the only one here that speaks good English except you."

I said, "Well, I not going to learn Cheyenne. I won't be here long enough."

Manda said, "Annie, Moree'e has made you some clothes. Please be polite and try them on and thank her for all her work. There are also moccasins in the pile as well as some deerskin boots for winter. She'll also bring you a jacket for winter as well as gloves and blankets. She is our major seamstress."

I looked all the things over and was very happy. I knew I was a mess. My dress now was almost in tatters and they took my boots away from me after I kicked the Nose in her knee. I smiled and went over and hugged Moree'e, and said, "Thank you Little Woman, this was so nice of you. I hope you don't mind me calling you by your English name."

Little Woman smiled and said, "Man…ny tanks. Ise glad." I went into the tepee and put on the deerskin dress and it was a perfect fit. The moccasins also were perfect. I was so happy, just maybe things were looking up.

After I was dressed like all the locals, Manda and I took a walk. As we strolled by the other women, they all stopped and stared. The whispering continued. Manda stopped in her tracks and looked at my face. She then said, "Follow me."

We walked to the edge of the encampment and she turned and looked at my face again, but this time with the sun shining on me. She said, "You are a beauty. I didn't realize that when you had that dirt all over you. You have stunning brown eyes and that black hair is now beautiful after it was washed. And those freckles all over your nose and cheeks are so cute. I don't think you know this, but you also have a dimple on both your cheeks. The braves will be fighting over you someday."

I smiled at her comments and I was a bit embarrassed. No one in my short life had ever said I was a beauty. My brothers called me mule face and many other unflattering names. I said, "Thanks, I've never seen my face before. I did see a reflection in a pond once, but my brothers jumped in and splashed the water around before I could make out what I looked like."

Manda said, "Come with me."

We slowly walked back to her tepee and went in. She had me sit down on some blankets and she handed me what she called a mirror. I looked at myself for the first time in my life. I liked what I saw. She was right, I am cute. I do have dimples and lots of freckles, dark brown eyes and black hair. I think I look a lot like Mommy.

Manda said, "Well, what do you think? You're pretty darn cute, aren't you?"

I was a bit embarrassed but I did say, "Yeah, I like my looks. But as far as the braves fighting over me someday, that will never happen. I'm not staying here very long, and I'd kill anyone of them that tries to touch me. Please don't think I don't appreciate what you've done for me, because I do. But I don't want any of these men. Keep in mind, they killed my family and I intend to kill them, including your son."

Manda replied, "We'll see, we'll see. I have a feeling you'll change your mind after a while."

CHAPTER SEVEN

Crow & The Nose

Early one morning a wagon came into the camp just as everyone was stirring. Driving the team was a man that was clearly of Indian descent. I concluded he was a handsome man by Indian standards. When his wagon stopped the entire tribe congregated near his wagon. You could feel the excitement in the air. I tugged at Manda's arm and said, "Who is that and why is everyone so excited?"

Manda took my hand and we walked away from all the excitement. She said, "His name is Standing Crow, or just Crow and he was once a member of our tribe. His father was Okohkeso, or White Crow and he was our War Chief. His mother was a white woman, and her name was Motohavae or Pitiful Woman. She died while trying to run away from the tribe. Crow was only a boy of fourteen when he left that night to try and find her. He found her body after searching these hills for over four months. He knew it was her from the clothes that were on the skeleton. He buried her remains where he found them and set out to try and find the men that killed her. He found what he thought were her killers many miles away from our camp, sitting peacefully by a fire, drinking moonshine. They were all drunk. He waited until the next morning before confronting them. He walked into their camp with only his bow and arrows as his weapons. The three men were awake and were very hungover. I'll try and explain to you what Crow told me about the encounter."

"Crow shouted at them, 'Who killed my mother? Which one of you drunks did that to my poor mother?' Now Crow spoke English, his mother insisted that he learn it because she was always planning on taking him away from us. One of the miners named Davy said, 'We didn't kill no one, son, we're just a couple of down-on-their-luck-old-miners. We done been here for over five months trying to get some nuggets out of this here creek. Please put the damn bow and arrow down and come over and have something to eat. We mean you no harm.'"

"Crow was confused from the warm reception he got from the miners. Maybe he found the wrong men. He said, 'Did you ever see an Indian woman walking in these hills? She would have been in a big hurry.'"

"Davy said, 'No son, we didn't see no Injun woman. But if she was done killed by some bad men, we'd gladly help you find them. Come over and warm yourself by our fire.'"

Manda continued, "Now, Crow liked the men and sat with them and told them his story. His mother was taken when she was sixteen by the Cheyenne and was married off to White Crow. She hated her life and the only thing that mattered to her was her son Crow. She felt Crow was old enough at the time to take care of himself, so she left. His father White Crow was killed in battle a year earlier and all the braves were lining up to marry Motohavae. She was a very pretty woman even though she was in her late thirties. She would have none of their advances, so she snuck away late one night."

I was stunned. I said, "She got away from here but was killed by some other tribe? I guess it's hard to get out of here, but I will. Mark my words, I will."

Manda quickly responded, "It wasn't another tribe that killed her, it was white men. Davy, Crow and the two others, Phil and Lenny left the camp and followed the creek down the hill. It took several days to find the culprits that killed Motohavae. Crow and his new friends came upon the four miners in the early morning. Davy and his men had pistols and rifles with them, the other miners had no weapons except knives. Davy asked the miners if they had seen an Indian woman around those parts. They all laughed and said, "We did find one around these parts a few months back and we treated her real well, didn't we boys? She provided us with some real comfort, if you get my meaning?"

"Davy raised his pistol and shot the man in the face. The three others stood up immediately and began to run. Crow shot two of the men in their backs with arrows. They didn't die by the arrows. Lenny shot the other man in the back of his head. Davy told Crow to take his time with the two with the arrows in their backs. He and his men walked out of earshot as Crow finished them off. Crow would never say what he did to them."

Manda continued, "Davy and his friends looked around the camp and found nothing but a still. You know, it's used to make moonshine? That still changed Crow's life. The three miners showed Crow how to make moonshine and that's what he does now; makes moonshine."

I asked, "Are Davy and the other miners still in Crow's life? It seems to me that they were all very close."

Manda replied, "I'm not sure where they all went. But all I know is that Crow was taught the moonshine business by them. I hope they stayed in contact with each other. Crow looked at Davy as a father figure, he always said he loved and respected him."

I replied, "I know all about shine, as my daddy used to called it. He was a drunk and because of his drinking he was responsible for my mommy and my brothers being killed. Does he sell that stuff to the tribe? Do they go crazy like my daddy did?"

"Yes, it's a problem. Thank God that they can only buy the stuff a couple of times a year. Let's go back and I'll introduce you to Crow. He's a nice man. He was married but she passed away a couple of years ago."

As Manda and I were walking back to where the festivities were taking place, I saw a shadow moving towards us. I looked up and there was the Nose, she was limping towards me with her arm raised in the air while holding a very large knife. Manda saw her too and she pushed me away and I ducked and rolled to the ground as the Nose tried to stab me. The knife grazed my shoulder and tore my top as I rolled over on to my feet. Nose was raging with anger and she was bent over ready to attack again. Out of nowhere, a hand grabbed mine and placed a small craving knife in it. I looked up and it was Crow. He smiled and said in English, "Be careful little one. Keep in mind she's old and slow and can't move very fast."

I was scared out of my mind before Crow slid that knife into my hand, now I was petrified. I never experienced a lack of confidence before, but I had none now. Here I was, a little girl facing a crazy Injun woman with a knife. I tried to reason with her, I quietly said, "Please Miss Nose, I'm sorry, I'm sorry." Now I knew she didn't understand me, but I thought if I showed remorse she might back down. She didn't. She attacked again. She swung wildly at my head with the knife and I ducked underneath it and it breezed an inch away from a direct hit to my forehead. Her swing made her trip and fall on top of me and the blade of the knife in my hand accidentally buried into her shoulder. She rolled over and tried to stand up for a few seconds before crumbling to the ground screaming in pain. She laid there screaming at me with the knife still embedded in her shoulder. I stood quietly in shock. I just stabbed someone and I'm only eleven years old. It was an accident, but I didn't think the tribe would see it that way. I thought for sure they'd kill me.

Manda walked over to me and said, "This is not good Annie. You've hurt one of us. I'll try and explain what happened before with you and Nose, but it may not make any difference."

Avonaco stared at me and began to yell at me. His mother was at my side and was explaining something to him I couldn't understand. All the tribal members wanted to get their hands on me. Manda stood in their way. Finally, Crow screamed something, and they all stop talking and yelling. He addressed Avonaco and was quite animated with hand gestures and his voice. Finally, Avonaco said something to his mother and he and several of the elders walked into a tepee.

Manda said to me, "You're one lucky little lady. They were going to kill you, but Crow has offered to buy you for some moonshine. The elders are making the final decision now. I know these men will not pass up a chance to get free moonshine. You'll go with Crow. He's a good man and he will take care of you. This is the best thing that could happen to you."

Manda was correct, Crow had purchased me for two gallons of shine. He walked over to me and said, "Little Miss Annie, I was told by Manda your name is Annie. I'm Crow. I'm going to take you home with me. Please do not be afraid, I won't hurt you." I got onto his wagon and we rode away. I turned back to watch the commotion that was taking place at the camp. Nose was being carted off to a tepee to get medical attention and the men were very happy with the extra shine they got for me. Just shows you what a life is really worth. Two gallons of shine.

CHAPTER EIGHT

MR. CROW OR DAD

Mr. Crow and I rode for hours in that old rickety wagon. The horse named Old Ned was pulling the wagon and he appeared to be as old as the wagon, if not older and just as rickety. Mr. Crow, as I called him was very nice. He asked about my family and I went into details about their demise. He understood completely my sorrow as his mother had gone through a similar experience when she was young. He also had met other women that the tribe had kidnapped over the years. Since his mom had gone through all the same things, he was very sympathetic with what they all had endured.

I asked what happened to his wife, and he replied, "She was killed by some very bad men. My little daughter Fanny was also killed by those same men. Fanny was only ten, about your age."

I was so sad at what he had said, so I told him, "Mr. Crow I'm so sorry about your family. I do know what it's like to lose your family. I didn't like my daddy, but I loved my mommy and my brothers."

Crow responded, "Yes, it's hard to go on after losing them. You see, I lost my mom after my father died, which he was no loss to me at all. He was a mad man. He hated everyone, including me. I think he resented the fact that my mom was white. He had several other wives that were all of Indian descent and he liked all his boys, but not his girls. He was the war chief, which means in the Cheyenne nation when all the tribes go to war, he was in charge. My guess is there are about three to four thousand Cheyenne in this Montana area. There are about twelve separate Cheyenne tribes that make up the Cheyenne nation. You were found by one of the tribes, the same tribe my father and mother belonged to."

I smiled at him and said, "Why are daddies so mean and so stupid? My daddy was mean, but he was also a drunk. He's the reason we left and came out west. My mommy knew he killed Mr. James and that is why we had to move."

Crow smiled back at me, he said, "Little Annie, you have had some tough times too, but you and I will get through them. I like you. I hope you like me, and you will become my daughter."

"I do like you too Mr. Crow and I hope you'll still like me after you get to know me better. Mommy always said I was a handful."

Crow laughed at my handful comment. He said, "I saw you in action back with the tribe with Big Nose. Manda had told me a little bit about you and your mom was correct, you are a handful. That old Big Nose is not well liked in that tribe. Her father was the damn peace chief in that tribe, and everyone had to kiss her ass when he was alive. I'm sorry. I shouldn't swear around you. You sure handled that crazy bitch though. Damn, there I go again with the damn swearing."

I began to giggle uncontrollably; I just couldn't stop. I finally said, "I've heard a lot worse swearing from my mommy. And my daddy, he couldn't say anything without swearing. So, don't say you're sorry, I like it when people swear."

Old Ned was working pretty hard getting up the big hill in front of us. I knew he was working hard because he farted all the way up. Crow said, "We're almost home. Did you notice Old Ned started moving a little faster when we got closer to our hill."

I replied, "No, I didn't notice, I actually thought he'd slowed down a bit. Old Ned couldn't beat me in a race, and I've got pretty short legs."

When we reached the top of the hill, I realized there were many trees around a small log cabin. There was a good-sized log barn too, quite a distance from the cabin. Two dogs ran to greet us with both wiggling their butts and their tails. Crow jumped down and scratched and wrestled with both of them. He said, "Annie, get down here and meet the rest of our family. This black guy is Moon and this brown guy is Shine. Boys, this here is your new sister, little Annie."

I jumped down and both the dogs ran to greet me. They whimpered, cried, wiggled and licked me. This was the best thing I could have asked for. I always wanted a dog, but Daddy said we couldn't afford to feed it. Crow said, "Follow me and I'll show you around."

We first went into our log cabin and I loved what I saw. I couldn't believe that there were two separate bedrooms. Crow told me I'd have my own bedroom; it had been his daughter Fannie's room. He was sure Fanny would be happy that someone as nice as me would have it. My goodness, my own bedroom with a bed in it. I had to sleep on our dirt floor and on the ground with my three brothers with all of us sharing the same blankets. My own bedroom, with a damn bed! There was a small kitchen and a wood stove for cooking. There was also a stone fireplace outside my bedroom. To my surprise there was even a window in the main room. I had only seen and slept in a mud huts before and that was only just a few times. The rest of the time it was outdoors on the ground. The cabin was clean and wonderful. Both dogs were allowed in the cabin but they had to stay by the door. They were not allowed in the main part of the cabin. I knew I'd change that rule immediately. I wanted those dogs in my bedroom.

As we were walking around, I noticed a creek running alongside Crow's property. I looked where it was running and to my surprise it was quite wide, and it ran down the hill and emptied into a small lake at the bottom of the hill. Crow said, "This is where we get our water.

It's fresh water and it is where I also get the water for my still." After the tour of our water supply and our cabin we walked towards the barn.

Before we got to the barn, I saw a small, tall building. It was the funniest building I'd ever seen. I asked Crow, "What is this building for?"

Crow smiled and said, "It's an outhouse. You know where you poop and pee."

I opened the door and laughed hysterically. I said, "I can't believe this, a house to poop and pee in. I never saw a house like this before. I think I'll like it better than pooping and peeing in the woods."

We then walked to the barn, both of us were laughing all the way. Once inside the barn I realized it was the largest barn I'd ever seen. I wondered why we would have such a large barn with only one horse. I soon found out why; we are moonshiners. Over half the barn was set up to make moonshine. Crow said, "Our business is making moonshine. I don't care if you come around while I'm working but please never come in here without me. I'll show you everything about making moonshine, but it can be dangerous. So please, just come in here when I'm around."

"I promise you I will always do as you say. Well, most of the time I will. Sometimes I just can't help myself. But that one rule I promise you I'll keep."

CHAPTER NINE

A Home at Last

Beginning to live with Crow was not without issues. But good issues. He treated me so nice and was so attentive to me. The main concern in his life was now my happiness. In my short life no one had treated me like this. He was always asking if I had enough to eat, was I happy, was there anything I wanted? And I never treated anyone in my life as good as I treated him. We were very happy together. The only thing I didn't like, was when he went on what he called his 'sales trips.' He was afraid to take me along and made me stay at home with Moon and Shine. Now, I love my dogs so much, but I get lonely without Crow around. Oops, I just referred to him Crow. I stopped calling him Crow after a month of living with him. I now called him Pa, Dad, Father or Daddy. To him any of the four were satisfactory, he hated it when I called him Crow. Occasionally, I do call him Crow but it is only when I'm a little mad at him, which was not often. Dad had showed me where to hide in case strangers or a wild animal were to come into our home. In my bedroom, there is a trapdoor that opens to a small crevice just big enough for me and Moon and Shine to slide down. Once down in the crevice, there is a small room just big enough for the three of us. I can bolt the trapdoor once we're inside. Dad explained that Fanny and his wife Millie were outside when the men came upon them. He said they had no chance to get into the hideout. So, when Dad left for a sales trip, I stayed close to our cabin with my two dogs.

After a couple of months of complaining that I hated being left alone, he relented and took me on what he thought would be a civilized trip. Now I forgot to say that Dad had several weapons for our home protection and some for his travels. He had given me a small Pocket Colt that he said was a percussion pistol. It was smaller than the big pistols Dad carried but it was so small I could shoot it. It had six shots and Dad and I practiced daily. It was fun and I loved it when I hit the targets. Dad never missed. He also had several percussion rifles that he shot daily. They were too big for me and too heavy. When I asked him where he got so many guns he just replied, "Don't ask."

Dad told me we lived somewhere in southern Montana almost near the middle of the Territory. There were some ragtag towns that he visited, and he sold shine to miners, to saloons and individuals. We made our dogs Moon and Shine, stay at home when we left on our trip. I was very anxious to see where Dad went and who he sold the shine to. After experiencing all that I saw on the trip, I regretted going. Also, it was very dangerous.

We headed straight west through some hills, through some rivers and creeks and also prairie. It appeared to me that Old Ned was dragging his ass, but Dad said he was just saving his energy. I just couldn't agree with that. If Old Ned was farting, he would be moving as fast as he could. He wasn't farting today, and I was worried he may die on us. Dad just laughed when I told him that, his reply was, "Old Ned is younger than you, he just looks old."

I was laughing so hard I thought I'd pee in my pants. I said, "Younger than me? He's got to be twenty-five. Who told you he was so young?"

"I bought him as a young colt about nine years ago. I know how old he is. If you worked as hard as Ned does, you'd look old too. Now, behave, you're hurting his feelings."

He was now laughing as hard as I was and he quietly said, "Now I have to pee."

We had so much fun riding along together and I wondered why we hadn't done this before. Within the next two minutes I found out why. Two riders came up to us from the west and I could see Dad reaching for his six gun. They both stopped when they reached our wagon. I looked them over and I knew they were trouble. The one with the long beard said, "Howdy neighbor, whatcha got in the back of that wagon? It wouldn't be moonshine, would it?"

Dad quickly said, "I ain't your neighbor and I don't have no moonshine. I suggest you two boys be on your way."

The two riders just sat on their horses and smiled at me. The bearded one said, "Ain't she a cutie. I bet she could warm a man up on a cold night."

In one second after the man said, 'warm a man up on a cold night,' they were both dead. I couldn't hear anything for quite a while. The gunshot was so loud it hurt my ears. Dad hugged me and said, "Baby, are you, all right? Those men were going to try and take you away and kill me, I had to take them out immediately. I'm so sorry you had to see this. We'll go back home now."

I got off the wagon and looked at these two sleazy old men. One was on the ground and the other was still slumped over in his saddle. The one on the ground had the smallest little pistol in his waistband. I reached down and took it out and said to Dad, "Look Dad, isn't this the smallest pistol you've ever seen?"

Dad looked me over and said, "Aren't you upset?"

I replied, "No, should I be? These were bad men, and they were going to hurt us. Why should I care if they're dead? I get to keep the little gun, don't I? Let's see what else they have that's worth keeping."

Dad said, "You are something else, yeah, you get the little pistol and I get the big boy guns. You asked me where I got all my guns, this is where, from men that try and rob me."

"Look at this Dad, a watch."

"Yes, it is. But look at what was in that fool's pocket, gold nuggets. Step aside, I'll look in the others pockets too."

Dad found several more nuggets in the other man's pockets and a few more in their saddle bags. Dad unsaddled both their horses and tied them to the back of the wagon. He said, "We can use these horses around our cabin. The smaller one will be yours."

"Gees Dad, I like traveling with you."

Dad sat on the wagon and looked sad. He replied, "Annie, this is a very dangerous place to live. Besides fools like this, there are the Indians. Now, they let me travel freely through their country because I'm one of them, but you are not. Also, the tribes want young women, and you know why. That's why I want to train you to shoot and to shoot quickly, just like I did today. Shoot and ask questions later. Got it? We have to be careful and this is the last trip I'm going to take you on."

I pouted for a couple of hours and I didn't talk to him until we stopped at a makeshift little village. He asked, "Are you going to be mad at me for the rest of my life?"

I replied, "No! I wish I could be, but I can't. I love you too much to be mad at you for that long."

I looked at Dad and he was crying. He quietly said, "You'll never know how much I love you too? Please don't ever stay mad at me." We hugged and got off the wagon and went into a mud hut to sell some moonshine.

CHAPTER TEN

SALES TRIP CONTINUES

Dad and I had been gone for three weeks when we entered a Cheyenne camp at the far end of our western excursion. As we rode in, many of the tribal members came out to greet us. They all stared at me and I supposed they were all wondering where Dad had gotten me. I could see that they all liked Dad really well but were a bit suspicious of me. After selling what was left in our wagon, Dad took me over to an Indian squaw and began bartering with her. She stood up and looked me over like she was measuring me. She grunted and groaned a bit and then shook her head up and down indicating yes. Dad said, "She thinks she has something you'll want."

I asked, "What's going on? What does she have that I want?"

Dad answered, "She has clothes, white women clothes. She also has winter clothes and warm boots, mittens and a hat. Winter will be here soon, and I want you to stay warm."

I almost cried. My dad is so good to me. He took me along on this trip so he could get me clothes and winter gear. And white women clothes too.

The Indian woman came out of her tepee with two dresses, a shawl, a sweater, a night gown, a bearskin robe, a hat, mittens, leather boots and underwear. Now I had never wore underwear in my entire life. Well, if you call a diaper underwear, I guess that last statement was incorrect. Mommy said underwear was a cost we couldn't afford. I had left all my new clothes that Manda had given me at her camp. Dad said, "Now you'll stay warm this winter and in case a nice boy comes around you'll look really good for him too."

"I don't like boys that way. I told you I had three brothers and all they did was tease me and make me cry. Well, I didn't cry but they made me mad."

We headed for home after being on the road for close to a month. Dad said this was the longest trip he ever been on. He hoped our dogs would be in good shape. The dogs had a small entryway into the barn to sleep and we did leave some food in there too. The dogs always hunted, so Dad thought they'd be alright. It took us over two weeks to return home after riding almost straight through. Waiting for us was only one dog, Shine. We searched all over our homestead for Moon, but we never even found his body. I felt so bad, I loved that dog so much. Seems like everything I love dies.

Dad told me we would have to get another dog, maybe two more. We needed dogs to alert us to dangers. Dad left a week later and headed for a homestead where he had gotten both Moon and Shine. Shine and I just stayed close to the cabin when Dad was gone. He returned with two dogs and an arm full of books. The books were for me to learn to read and write and the dogs were for both of us. One of the dogs was a puppy we called Moon Two and the full-grown dog we called Eagle. I had so much fun with that little puppy Moon Two and I finally just called him Moon.

Winter was quickly approaching, and we needed to get ready. Dad was cutting down dead trees in our forest and was splitting them into logs for the fireplace to keep us warm. He already had a large stack of firewood by the cabin, he was just making sure we had enough. Dad had also made jerky and steaks from the deer he shot on the prairie near our homestead. With hunting for rabbits, squirrel and birds we'd have enough food. The dogs had gotten to know one another and got along very well. Moon was the baby and he couldn't stop jumping and trying to play with the older dogs, however, they just tried to ignore him.

Winter hit us hard up on that hill and we were forced to stay close to the cabin. Dad and I worked hard to clear all the snow away from the cabin, but we just let it pile up around the barn. Dad did keep the entryway to the barn cleared, however. Even though the snow was deep, I played outside every day. Dad also insisted that I work on my reading and writing every day. He was also very good at arithmetic, which he learned from an old trapper named Ted Boran. The winter was a very nice time for me. There was no stress, just happiness being with Dad and my dogs. It was a winter I'd never forget.

CHAPTER ELEVEN

THE GRIZZ & NEW MOM

Spring was here in 1869. I had been with Dad for around four years, and I think I'm now around fourteen years old. I might add this was best four years of my life. It was now around the end of May, and finally all the snow had melted but it was still pretty cold at night. Dad was back to making his moonshine and deliveries. But for some reason, this time he left Old Ned and the wagon at home and just mounted his horse and left. He said he was making social visit. My job while he was gone was to tend to the gardens, clean up the barn and work on my reading and writing skills.

My four-legged friends were always with me and would let me know if any black bears, grizzly bears or bad men were coming after us. The work was hard, but I was getting bigger and stronger now. Dad said he thought I was over five feet tall, I however, laughed at him, because I knew I'd be about six feet tall. Being short just didn't run in my family. Everyone was tall and skinny, including my daddy.

In my four years on top of that hill, which we called home, we never had any intruders venture up here, that all changed one morning several days after Dad had left on his social trip.

Now, I must explain a few things about our cabin. Dad had installed big wooden bars inside both the door and on our only window. There were two wooden bars on the door, that I was told emphatically must be put in place at nighttime. Dad installed strong wooden shutters on the inside of our window with a large bar to make sure no one could enter it at night. I also had that trap door with my little hiding place below the cabin. When Dad was gone, I felt very safe with the door and window barred and my three dogs with me inside.

One early morning, I was awakened by some noise at our window. The day before I had killed two quail and cooked them for my dogs and me. It was so good and smelled so good too. However, that smell must have permeated throughout the woods. The scratching sound at our window woke the dogs and me. The dogs barked and whimpered at the door, wanting to get out and attack.

I didn't know what to do, at first. I reached for my small pistol and walked out of my bedroom and told my dogs to shut up, which they did. The scratching and the growling sounds didn't stop. So, I also grabbed one of Dad's larger six shooter and set it down near me and pulled up the bar on the window and opened the shutters. There in front of me was the face of a big hungry grizzly bear looking for food. When a grizz comes out of hibernation, they will eat anything they can find, and they need to find it right away. Just think about it, they've been starved for several months. As the grizz stuck his head further in the window, I quickly shot him in his face six times. He jumped back and was wiping and slapping at his face like he was being attacked by bees. I realized then I may have blinded him. I ran for the door with the big six shooter in my hand and took off the two bars and followed the dogs out. The bear was going crazy and stood up on his hind legs as the dogs attacked. The bear could not see where the dogs were, and he just swung his claws everywhere he heard a bark or a growl. I walked straight up to him and I was about six or seven feet away. He must have smelled me because he turned to face me. I pointed Dad's six shooter and fired six shots into his chest. He fell forward attempting to slash me with his claws as he fell. He died immediately when he hit the ground. This large bear almost landed on top of me and one of his claws nicked me on the side of my cheek. There I stood with a dead grizz at my feet. I was bleeding a bit and I was also bit shaken. The dogs were still going wild, barking and chomping on the grizz. I finally got up enough nerve to look at what I had done and I stepped back a few feet.

After taking some deep breaths, I thought about what Dad had always said, 'If someone tries to break in let them try. If they can break down that door or window, shot um if they get in.' I guess I shouldn't have opened that damn window. But I killed a grizz, not many women have ever done that. I'm so proud of myself but I wonder if Dad will feel that way too? I hope so.

I knew I had to do something with the grizz's body. Dad told me long ago we don't waste meat. So, I had to gut this big beast right away. I needed to roll it over on his back. But how in the hell does a girl that weighs about sixty-five pounds do that to a six-hundred-pound bear? She gets her horse and her three dogs to help.

I tied a rope around the grizz's paws and legs and tied the rope to Old Ned. Ned was pretty shy at first when I brought him close to the grizz. But he settled down a bit after the dogs showed him, they were not afraid. It just took a few of minutes of shouting at Ned to get the bear on his back. I knew Ned was working as hard as he could by all the farting he was doing. Gees, does he smell.

After the grizz was on his back I began to gut him. Over the last couple of years, I had gutted many deer and a few elk but never a grizz or a black bear. Dad said he didn't really like the taste of bear meat. After butchering this guy, he'd better develop a taste for at least grizz. This bastard is so big.

After I got all the innards out of the bear, I gave the dogs the heart and liver and it appeared that was all they wanted. The rest I hauled away in the wheelbarrow. I took me five loads of innards to haul away from that grizz. But I was finally able to get all the waste well out of the area of our home and into the woods. When I got done with the gutting, I was dead tired. I covered the bear with a tarp Dad used on the wagon and left the grizz where it laid. Tomorrow I'd work on him again.

At daybreak there was a hard knock on the door. I woke very tired and very startled. At first, I thought maybe it was Madam Grizz looking for Mister Grizz. That notion left my mind immediately when I heard Dad yell, "Annie are you in there? Annie are you, all right?"

I opened the door and there was Dad standing with a pretty woman. Dad looked me over and said, "What in the hell has gone on around here, are you alright? Who killed the grizz?"

I looked the woman over and said, "Who are you?"

Dad said, "Annie, answer my questions."

I nonchalantly said, "I killed it. He was trying to get into the house, so I shot him. I did get his innards gutted but I think I'm too small to butcher him myself." I looked at the lady again and said, "Who are you?"

The lady responded, "I'm a friend of your dad's. My name is Sue Stands-Alone. Your dad and I have known each other for a few years now and we love each other. I'm here to live with you two, if that's okay with you?"

I stood there in shock. I had no idea Dad had a girlfriend, he never mentioned anyone, especially not her. I didn't know how to respond. I finally said, "I really don't have anything to say about this matter. Crow never told me he had a girlfriend. You can stay as far as I'm concerned, it appears I don't have any say in anything around here any longer."

Dad said, "Annie, answer me about the damn bear. Did you not do as I told you? You were never to open that damn door or window to any person or animal."

I was getting mad, I yelled, "Listen Crow, if you were here protecting us, I wouldn't have had to go after that intruder by myself. I opened that damn window and shot the son-of-a-bitch. I shot him six times in the window and another six times in the yard. Sorry if that bothers you now Crow, but you weren't here, so I did what I had to do."

"Listen Annie, I'm not Crow to you, I'm Dad, nothing more, nothing less. I expect you to treat Sue with kindness and respect. She is going to be your mother."

I smiled before saying, "My mom is dead, and this person here will never be my mom. I'm leaving here today."

Sue walked over to me and then turned to Crow and asked him to go outside and to leave us women alone. After he had left, Sue said, "Annie, I'm not a replacement for your mom. I never expected to be that person. I had only hoped we could have become friends and have a nice relationship. I told Crow that I should have met you first and gotten to know you before springing me moving in on you. My intention was not to surprise or make you uncomfortable. This is your home, and I can understand you view me as an intruder. I'll leave here now, and I promise I won't come back. This is your home and not mine. It was nice meeting you Annie, all of what Crow told me about you is true; you are a beautiful, strong young woman and I like you. Goodbye Annie."

Sue turned and began to walk out the door when I stopped her. I said, "Please don't leave. I didn't give you much of a chance, did I? I think the thought of sharing my dad with someone really hurt me. I'm sorry I was such a spoiled brat. I like you too and you would make a nice mom. Please forgive me and please stay." Besides being so nice, she is really pretty. I think I was just being a brat because I thought Dad would be mad about me killing the grizz. I never gave her a chance. Now I had to face Dad.

Sue said, "Would you mind showing me that grizz you killed. You are one tough little cookie."

CHAPTER TWELVE

HOMESTEAD

The first night that Sue stayed with us, I woke up screaming very loudly. I had a nightmare that I was being clawed by a giant grizz. My screaming woke Sue, but my dad never heard me. Sue rushed into my room and grabbed me tightly and stroked my hair. She quietly said, "It's alright Annie, everything is alright. You just had a bad dream."

I held onto Sue like I've never held onto anyone in my life. It was so comforting having a woman hold me again like my mom used to do. I said, "Sue would you sleep with me tonight?"

Sue smiled and replied, "Of course sweetie, I'll do anything you ask of me."

Boy, did that make me feel good. It felt like I had a mom again. The next morning, I woke with Sue lying wide awake in the bed beside me. She said, "You are such a pretty young lady. I've been watching you sleep for over an hour and it has been so much fun being here with you. I was never able to have children, so lying here next to you has been a big treat for me."

I smiled at her and said, "Thanks for being here for me last night. I don't know what happened to me. I've never woke up in the middle of the night like that before. Even after my family were all killed, I didn't have nightmares. But I guess that grizz did scare me a bit. But when I was shooting it, well I was as calm as could be. I just don't understand what happened to me. Why weren't you able to have kids?"

Sue replied, "I'll tell you all about that later. You are a very determined, strong young lady and I think after the shooting you probably had exhausted yourself. Are you hungry? Let's go eat."

We went out to our little kitchen and Sue cooked up some oatmeal for us. Dad had finally gotten up and was drinking a large cup of the coffee Sue had also made. So, I asked, "What about the babies?"

Sue laughed and said, "You are an inquisitive young lady, aren't you? Okay, here goes; my mom and dad and my aunt and uncle and I, all traveled west so the men could pan for gold. My dad just up and died while panning for the gold one day. All of us were living inside a tent. After we buried Dad, Mom wanted to get far away from that damn creek that she figured had killed Dad. We left Aunt June and Uncle Herb at the creek and we began to walk. We walked east for several days when your dad found us. We had run out of food and water and we were dead tired and lost. Crow helped my mom into the wagon, and he took us to a small settlement called Settlers Gulch. Now the Gulch has nothing but sod huts, not like your home here. Mom had a few silver coins left and offered them to a man named Rocky Stands-Alone to let us stay with him. Rocky was a half breed, part Indian part white. His daddy was an Indian and his mommy was a white woman. He had two kids and no wife. His wife and her baby died in childbirth. Eventually, Rocky wanted to marry me but since there was no one to marry us we just lived together as husband and wife. Well, Rocky was finding gold nuggets every day and was hiding them away from me. One day he packed up the kids and left. He never told me was leaving, he just left one morning. I didn't realize he was gone until around noon, after I had tended to our garden. So, while I was with Rocky, I never was able to get pregnant, so I always thought I was sterile. Sterile is not being able to have babies."

I said, "Wow, what a story. Did you like the kids, and did you love Rocky?"

Sue thought for a second before saying, "I didn't like his kids and they didn't like me. They were older and they thought I was trying to replace their mother, which I was not. They were just downright mean to me. It was kind of like when I met you yesterday, but I liked you right away. I never loved Rocky; it was just a relationship of convenience for both of us. I realized that I was being used for sex and to care for him and his kids. A friend of mine in our little village told me about Rocky's deceit in hiding his gold. I was left with nothing. Your dad would stop by often and he hired me to make clothes for him to sell. That's when we began our love for one another."

I said, "Well, I like you and I'm happy to have another person around here to keep Dad in line. Also, I'll need your help skinning that grizz and butchering it too."

Dad said, "The three of us will take care of the beast. We'll need to get some of that meat cooked immediately and dried. That skin will be worth a lot of money,"

Sue said, "Crow, that grizz is Annie's to do what she wants to do with it. And Annie, if you want the hide so be it. Also, I want the claws cut off, I have a plan for them, one I think you'll like Annie."

After breakfast we all went to work on that grizz. It was cut up and the hide was stripped off the carcass to dry and tan. Sue had Dad cut all the claws off and she scrubbed all of them. Dad was going to take some of the raw meat and sell it to some folks in the Gulch. Sue and I were cooking the meat over a pit in the yard and also, we cooked some in the kitchen. After Dad left, Sue took me into the cabin and explained what she was planning on doing with the claws.

Sue said, "Annie every brave that kills a grizz takes its claws and makes a necklace out of them. You see it's a very big thing to kill a grizz and a sign of extreme bravery. Not many survive an attack by a grizz. So, with that being said, you rank up there with the bravest of all warriors. Also, because you are small right now, I'm going to take one claw and make a necklace for you out of just the one. I will also make a big necklace out of all the other claws. You may want to wear the big necklace when you get bigger."

I was stunned. I had tears running down my cheeks. When I was finally able to talk, I said, "Are you for real? Why are you being so nice to me after the way I treated you?"

"Yesterday and last night was a real eyeopener for me. First, it was seeing that grizz you killed all by yourself. The courage it must have taken. And then, seeing you last night so sweet and needy, acting like a true fourteen-year-old little girl. You brought out all of my motherly instincts. I felt like finally someone really needed me."

CHAPTER THIRTEEN

FAMILY DANGERS

I loved having Sue living with us. I began to call her Mom now and I feel she's as good as my real mom was. I can see the love that Dad has for her. They laugh all the time and are constantly kissing and hugging one another. I never saw my real folks do anything like that. It must be real love. I like it. Also, I now wear a necklace with one bear claw on it. Mom says it sends a message to all men, don't pick on me.

Mom has been with us for over a year now and she asked me if I would step outside, she wanted to tell me something important. Of course, I did as she requested. She began, "Now, I hope you'll not be upset with what I'm going to tell you, but you're going to have a little brother or sister. I'm pregnant and will have a baby in about six months. I hope you're not upset about this."

I was stunned and I began to cry, which is something I seldom ever do. I said, "Are you crazy? This is what I was hoping would happen. I want a sister if possible, but I'll take a little brother too. Mom, I thought you couldn't have a baby, this is the best news I could ever hear. I love you so much and I so happy you'll have a baby of your own."

"Annie, it's going to be all of our family's baby. I feel that you are my own child too. This will just make our family a little bigger. Dad is so happy too."

I hugged her and told her how excited I was. Dad walked out of the cabin and said, "Do I get a hug too. I did have something to do with it too." I hugged Dad too and also told him how much I loved him.

Having Dad buy me from the tribe was the best thing that could have happened to me. I am so happy with where we live and with my family. I just wish Dad didn't have to travel so much. I also have asked him to give up the moonshine business, it's way too dangerous.

Things were going so well. Mom was doing great and she was very happy. She wasn't getting too big, but she told me that would come later. Dad had finished his last batch of moonshine and was going to take off and make some delivers. He told Mom and me that the demand for moonshine was the best it had ever been with all the miners panning for gold. Now the gold panning wasn't as big around here as it was further west, but every creek and river had miners working claims. Dad said, "The lazy bastards all want to forget their miseries in a jug of shine. Most of the miners that I see are dirt poor and down on their luck. They are down on their luck because they're lazy and always want to get rich quick off of someone else. They think that by putting a pan in a creek or river they'll strike gold right away. That's what they been told and that's why so many of these men are here. They are so stupid that they buy shine and not food, so they're starving to death too. Also, they don't realize until it's too late that the Indians don't want them on their land. I figure that in about six months they'll all be gone. I assume the ones that are still alive will move further west. So, I better sell as much of this shit as I can before there is no demand. I guess then I'll retire and stay home and babysit my two girls."

Dad left that morning and took our dogs Eagle and Moon with him. He said he was getting worried that these miners might try and attack him at night while he was sleeping. The dogs were along to warn him. He also told Mom and me to be careful around the homestead.

But Mom and I were not worried one bit. We hadn't had a visitor ever. Yes, I said ever. No one would ever look on top of this treed hill and expect to find someone living here. That's why Dad had picked this spot. How wrong we all were.

Early one morning, a week after Dad had left on his sales trip, three dirty men rode up our hill and entered our yard. Shine came after them barking and growling and spooking their horses. Two of the men were on the ground, while the one still in the saddle pulled out his six gun and shot Shine twice. One shot hit him in his side and the other in the head. He died immediately. One of the men on the ground yelled, "Everyone in that damn cabin get your asses out here now." Mom told me to hide under my bed, she'd go out. I did what she told me to do, but I first grabbed my small pistol and Dad's big six-shooter.

Mom walked out and frantically said, "Why would you shoot my dog and what do you want?"

The man on the horse slowly got down on the ground and said, "Are you that damn Crow's woman? We're here for moonshine, our gold and also some fun with you little lady. Where's the moonshine kept?"

Mom was shaking uncontrollably at the comments about fun with her. She looked the men over and she had never seen such poor excuses for men in her life. She finally said, "Please, take all the moonshine and whatever else you want but please leave me alone. I'm with child and I don't want to lose it. Please just leave me alone."

One of the men said, "Stan, let's just get the gold, the shine and some food and be on our way. What good would it do to hurt this little girl."

Stan answered, "Bobby, shut the hell up. Now girlie, you get that sweet ass of yours moving and show us the still. Lyle, you stay here and look for the gold and watch the horses. We'll give you a yell when it's your turn."

Lyle yelled, "Shit Stan, why am I always last? Why can't Bobby be last." Stan just stared and motioned for Bobby and Mom to move towards the barn.

As they were walking Stan grabbed Mom's butt and she turned and slapped him. He stood there alongside of her for a second and rubbed his face. He then slugged her in the face, and she went flying through the air. She landed on her back. Stan yelled, "If you ever do that again you'll be dead meat! Do you understand me? You now belong to us and we'll do whatever we want with you. Bobby, pick her up and drag her into that barn. Do it now!"

Back in the cabin, I slid out from under the bed. I knew my Mom was in trouble and she needed my help. I thought, '*I need to kill these bastards or die trying. I will not allow anyone to hurt my mom.*' After standing up in the bedroom, I looked out and saw the one called Lyle coming in. I had my guns hidden behind my back as he entered the cabin.

Lyle said, "Well, well, what do we have here? Another little lady that needs my attention." Lyle walked into the cabin and closed the door behind him. He smiled and said, "Come over here little darling, big Lyle has something I'm sure you'll want. Ain't you a cutie, I bet this will be your first time. After I'm done with you, I'll want you to show me where your daddy hid our gold."

I stood there as this filthy, dirty old man began to take down his trousers. I did wonder what he meant about my daddy hiding his gold. That confused me more than seeing this idiot take down his trousers. When he was standing in his long johns facing me, I brought both the guns in my hands around and pointed them at him. I calmly said, "What's your name big boy? I think I heard you call yourself Lyle. What gold were you asking about? But you won't need any gold where you're going. So, Lyle, what are you gonna do, your gun and holster are on the floor along with your trousers? Now you can try and pick it up and shoot me, but I don't think you're quick or smart enough to do that. But Lyle, you dumb shit, go for it."

"Listen here Missy, you ain't old enough to shoot a man. No sir, you ain't. Besides, I'll let you go if you tell me where our gold is hidden." After his comment, I shot him in what Mom called the groin area. He dropped to the floor crying his eyes out.

I said, "Lyle, Lyle, there's your gun lying next to you, go for it." He did and I shot him in the forehead. I then climbed out our window and ran around the back of the cabin.

Lyle's friends must have heard the shots. Bobby came running out of the barn and up to the cabin. He opened the door and looked inside and saw Lyle's body. As he turned to run back to the barn, he saw me standing in his path. He was fumbling trying to get his gun out of his holster when I shot him in his right shoulder. He dropped to the ground. I said, "You must be the person called Bobby. Goodbye Bobby and good luck in hell." I shot him in his head. I then ran into the woods.

I was behind a stand of maple trees watching what Stan was going to do. He walked out pushing Mom along in front of him. He saw Bobby and yelled, "Bobby, who did this to you? Bobby are you alright?" Obviously, he wasn't. Stan looked through the cabin door and saw Lyle lying face down in a pool of blood. He scratched his head as he was trying to figure out who had killed his friends. He screamed at Mom, "Who's doing this? Don't you lie, who killed my friends? Did that goddamn thieving Crow do this? Answer me dammit, answer me. I promise I'll kill you if you don't answer me."

Mom looked like she was in shock. I remember when I was in shock, it was after I was attacked by the Nose. This outlaw had a gun to Mom's temple and was shouting for whoever did the killings to come forward. I put the big pistol behind my back, and I walked slowly out of the woods. Stan saw me immediately. He looked confused. I'm guessing he couldn't figure how a kid, a little girl, could get the drop on his friends. He finally said, "Who did the killing here?"

I replied, "I don't know, I was in the woods looking for berries when I heard the shots. I thought it was you who shot everybody. Why are you holding my mommy like that? I think you're hurting her. Please let her go."

Stan quietly said, "Where's the man that shot my friends? Was it that lying, thieving, murdering son-of a-bitch Crow that did this, is he still around?"

I said in quiet, sympathetic tone, "I don't know where Crow is, but what I do know is that my mommy is very upset. Please let her go. If you don't, I'm sure that Crow will be very mad at you. I guess he already killed your friends. And, by the looks of things around here, I'm guessing he'll be coming after you next."

Stan laughed and spun Mom around so her back was facing him and he was holding her up by her ponytail. His backside, however, was now facing me. He said, "He'll have to shoot her first to get to me." He then yelled, "Come out you dirty, thieving son-of-a-bitch. Let's have it out right now. Come on!"

I quickly shot him in his butt. He dropped to his knees and let go of Mom. Mom ran to me and stood behind me. She said, "Are you all right Annie?"

I replied, "I couldn't be better." I then yelled at Stan, "Stan, please draw that gun of yours out of your holster. I'd like to make a gunfight out of this. Whaddya say big man. Are you going to let a little fourteen-year-old girl kill you? Go for it!" Stan tried in vain to get the six-shooter out of his holster. I shot him five more times before he died, and I laughed at him every time one of the slugs entered his body. He cried and pleaded with me to stop, but I didn't. Mom had to finally ask me to finish him off, which I did.

I quickly asked Mom if they had hurt her. She said "They were going to, but they heard the shots that were being fired and that must have worried them. That Stan said he thought that Lyle must have shot one of us, maybe Dad. Annie are sure you're alright? Did they hurt you? Did killing them upset you? I don't know if I could have done what you did. You are so strong."

"Mom, it doesn't bother me at all. Those men were going to hurt you and me. I couldn't let that happen. I was worried that I would be too late to stop them from hurting you. I will tell you one thing, the guy named Lyle was so stupid. He dropped his pants and gun on the floor. He wanted me for sex, I guess. But I had him for target practice. He was so stupid. He asked me where their gold was hidden. Do you know what gold he was talking about? What should we do with these bodies now?"

Mom said, "I have no idea about any gold. We don't have hardly any silver, let alone gold. Let's get one of those horses out of the corral and tie them up and drag their bodies into the woods. I'm not going to bury them, we'll let them rot in the woods and let the varmints feast on them. Good riddance, they deserved to die. We also should check their saddlebags and pockets for any loot. I doubt if they had much. You are the strongest little lady I've ever known. I love you so much."

Now, I'm sure you can understand why I love my mom so much.

CHAPTER FOURTEEN

BABY ADDIE-LOU

Dad got home and immediately knew something was wrong. First, he saw three more horses in the corral and wondered, where in the hell was Shine? He jumped down off his wagon and ran into the house, much to the surprise of Mom and me. He shouted, "Is everything all right and where is Shine?"

Mom quietly said, "Yes, things are alright now. But both Annie and I are putting our feet down about you leaving us alone again to sell moonshine. Shine was killed by some of your customers. They were going to rape me and Annie, but our dear daughter saved the day. That little girl killed all three of them. They're rotting in the woods now as we speak."

Dad quietly said, "I think both of you are right, I need to be here with you. I'm now out of the moonshine business. So, we lost Shine to some customers of mine and one of them was likely a guy called Stan. I had a run in with about six or seven men that were working a claim together. Bobby was his puppet and another guy named Lyle was his go to muscle guy. Lyle was rumored to be a killer. Fast with a gun and had no fear and no brains. But that Stan was both fearless and dangerous. I had a run in with them about a week ago and several times before. They wanted moonshine on credit, and I told them no. I had a fight with Stan, and I beat him up pretty good. After I left their camp, I wondered what they'd try and pull on me. I never thought they be able to find this place. I'm so sorry, and I promise, I'll be here from now on."

I had tears running down my cheeks when Dad came over and hugged me. He said, "You are the strongest little lady I've ever met, thank you for taking care of Mom and our homestead."

I said, "Thanks Dad, but Mom and I have a question of you. Two of those men asked us where their gold was hidden. They said you stole it from them, and they wanted it back. They also called you a murderer. They were going rape Mom and me and then make us tell them where the gold was hidden. Dad, do we have any gold?"

Dad shook his head and said, "Are you kidding me. Gold? We don't even have any silver coins let alone gold. We're poor. I have no idea what they were talking about. They tried to steal my moonshine that's all."

Mom said, "Sweetie, remember they wanted me to show them where the still was and where the moonshine was kept. I guess they must have thought Dad made a lot of money on the moonshine business."

I replied, "Mom, I think you are right. Those men were so dumb. They thought I was just some little girl that was afraid of them. Well, I showed them I'm not. I'd like you both to know that I had no trouble killing them. They all deserved to die. I wasn't afraid and it didn't bother me killing another human being. It was like killing that grizz, it had to be done. After the Nose tried to kill me, I lost my fear of most everything. But losing Shine will hurt me the most. I loved that dog so."

Mom strolled over to me and hugged me before saying, "There are so many men like Stan and his friends here in the west. They are lonely and they want a woman for comfort and for sex. I've tried to explain the sex thing to you, but it's difficult to understand at your age. A man's sex drive is so strong that sometimes they go crazy when they want a woman. That's when it's called rape. Men forcing a woman to have sex with them. The men you killed were that type of men and the only way to stop them is to kill them. If I would have had a gun, I would have killed them too. So, with that being said, you did nothing wrong, you just protected us. I've been raped before and it's a horrible cxperience. I didn't realize it at the time, but Rocky forced himself on me the first several times. One of his friends raped me too. I finally just gave into Rocky. You asked if I loved him, I not only didn't love him I hated him. It was such a relief when he and those horrible kids upped and left me."

After all the killings, Mom, Dad and I settled down for a few months and waited for our new family member to come along. It was such a nice time for me having Dad home all the time with Mom and me. We worked every day, cleaning the cabin, tending to our livestock and gardens. Dad and I hunted regularly for rabbits, fowl, moose and deer. Occasionally, we killed an elk and that was a big deal for us. Elk meat was the best. The only problem with killing an elk, was they were so big that we couldn't store all the meat. We made jerky out of most of it and since the winter months were upon us, we could freeze some of it too. We'd have elk meat for almost all of the winter, which would be nice. Dad and I had also cut and split enough firewood to last us the entire winter. Mom wanted to help with all the preparations for winter but was she not physically able to do so, being pregnant and all.

In the beginning of January, in the midst of major blizzard, Mom went into labor. She was screaming in pain and Dad and I didn't know what to do. Mom yelled at me, "Annie, you're going to have to help me, Dad is not capable. Please come in here and I'll try and explain what to do."

I walked into the bedroom and closed the door. Mom looked at me again and said, "Sweetie, I know you're able to do this, you are so strong. I'm going to scream in pain but ignore all my crying and screaming. You'll need to concentrate on helping get this baby out of me. Here comes the pain again that's good, it means the baby is ready to come out."

Mom screamed in pain and I tried to ignore it, but that was so hard. Watching someone you love go through all that was upsetting to say the least. Mom pushed and pushed and finally I saw the little bugger's head show up. Soon after that she slid out. I did say she; it was a little girl. Mom was happy but still in pain and she told me what to do next. I didn't have to turn the little bugger upside down and swat it's butt, because it was crying as soon as it hit the fresh air in the cold cabin. I had to cut the cord that was attached to Mom and Mom walked me through that. I washed the little bugger off with a damp clean rag and then wrapped it in a small blanket and handed her to Mom. She was smiling ear to ear. I wasn't, however. This was the hardest thing I'd ever been through.

Mom said, "Thank you sweetie for helping me and not panicking. I know this was hard on you."

I replied, "I don't think you should have another one of these. They're just too much trouble. I'll get Dad."

Dad came in and he was all googly-eyed over the new baby and was so proud of Mom. He asked, "What are we going to name her?"

Mom quickly answered, "Addie-Lou! Addie-Lou was my grandma's name, I want her to be just like she was. She was kind and such a wonderful lady, and I loved her so."

I replied, "I don't think this one will be like that. She was sure stubborn trying to get out and all she's done since she got out is cry. I don't like her, she's too much trouble."

Mom quietly said, "Annie Crow, how dare you talk about your little sister like that? Is it because she got all the attention around here today? Now you be nice to her, alright?"

"Alright, alright, I'll be nice to this little crybaby. I still don't like her, but I'll be nice," I said with a smile.

CHAPTER FIFTEEN

GOLD??

I have a new name for my little sister, I call her Assie-Lou. Now, I know I shouldn't dislike any member of my family, but she was hard to like. Mom and Dad gush over everything she does. If she lets a fart they laugh. When they changed her poopie diapers they laugh and when she cries, they run to her to see if wants the nipple. I am so sick of seeing Mom feed that kid and seeing her boobs out all the time. However, I finally realized what those things are for, feeding babies. I knew that shortly I'd have those damn things too; Mom had prepared me for them. I hope they'll be smaller than Mom's.

I stayed away from the baby as much as possible. I hunted daily and spent much of my time with the horses and my two dogs Moon and Eagle. When hunting, I took only Moon with me, he was a great hunter and never barked, except once.

I was hunting a long way from home, with the old rifle Dad had given me and I always carried my little pistol too. Dad had brought home a small holster for me to carry the pistol in and it also had a cartridge belt. The holster was very ornate with some kind of beading sewn on it. I now wore deerskin pants and a deerskin long top. I think I look more like an Indian than white girl. As Moon and I slowly walked through the woods, Moon stopped and began to growl. He then began to bark incessantly at something ahead of us. He ran ahead to attack whatever it was. I didn't follow him, as I thought there could be trouble brewing. When I say trouble, I mean a grizz or something like that. I was startled when I heard a gunshot and my dog cry and then wimpier. And then another shot. I hid behind some bushes and trees trying to see where the enemy was and who or what it was. I set my rifle down and reached for my pistol and held it steadily in my hand. I thought, *'Why am I not afraid? I can't believe I'm not. Is it because I just don't care? I think I do care. I don't want to die, I know that, but I will not let someone abuse me.'*

I heard some male voices talking, one said, "Where the hell do you think this dog came from? You think it was just a wild dog or his? Damn, it was a good-looking mutt, I'll say that for it."

The man said, "I don't give a shit if it was good looking or not, it's now a dead dog. I don't know if he has a damn dog. We need to get moving on, we need to find that son-of-a-bitch soon and before it gets dark."

The other man said, "Do you think we're close? When we find him, do you think he'll give up our gold?"

"He'll give us the gold and he'll die today. We know he has it, and it will soon be ours again."

"He's got that kid still, don't he? She's got to be of age now, don't she? You know a woman?"

"How in the hell should I know that? The last time I saw her she was just a little kid. Maybe she's a woman now. That'd be nice. Real nice."

"What direction should we head?"

"West, it's got to be west. Can you smell something cooking in the air?"

"No! I ain't smelled nothing. You're just hungry."

"I'm not hungry Jimmy, I just smell something in the air. Let's go this way."

"All right, we'll go that way. If we find him, we'll take our gold and kill um. He's gotta be dead after we get the gold back, I don't want him after us. He's a mad man."

I sat behind those bushes and thought about them killing Moon. What kind of man shoots a dog for no reason at all? Moon was just warning them not to come close to me. I swore I'd get even with them. I realized they must be after Dad too. But we didn't have any gold, at least that I knew about. I wondered, *'Did Dad have some gold that he never told Mom and me about?'* I couldn't confront them in the woods, but I'd follow them and see if they were after Dad. But who else could they be after, no one else lived around here that I knew of? If it is Dad, they're after, maybe I could help him out.

I followed them at a safe distance behind, well behind I might add. If these were Indians, they'd have known I was behind and tracking them. So, I was pretty sure it was just a couple of white men. Also, an Indian wouldn't be making so much noise. They were still talking loudly as they walked through all the brush. When they saw the smoke from our fireplace they quickly quieted down. As they crawled up closer to the cabin, Eagle must have smelled them and came running in their direction growling and barking. Dad came out of the cabin with his six shooter in his hand, looking around in the direction where Eagle was barking. He stood for a moment behind Eagle, looking around. Suddenly a shot was fired that hit Dad directly in his chest. He dropped immediately to the ground. I could see Mom in the doorway holding Addie-Lou. She had a look of fright on her face and she quickly closed the door and I assume she bolted it with wooden beams. I guessed she did the same to the window. I'd also hoped she went into my bedroom and slid her and Addie-Lou down in the little escape hole Dad had made for his previous family.

The two men walked up to Dad's body and shot another round into it. Eagle had scampered away. They then walked to the cabin door and shouted, "All right now Missy, we saw you and the kid. Open the door and nothing will happen to you. We just want what Crow stole from us, our gold. Come on now and be a good girl and open the door. If ya don't, we'll burn the whole place down with you in it, now you wouldn't want us to do that, would ya? You want the kid to live don't ya. Be a good girl and open that damn door."

There was no response from inside the cabin. I'm sure Mom was hidden in the escape hatch and she would never open that door, not with Addie-Lou there. I now wished I had brought my rifle with me. I forgot and left it by the tree in the woods. I had to figure out a way to get the drop on these killers.

One of the men banged on the door and screamed, "Listen you little bitch, all we want is our gold, the gold Crow stole from us. Open this fuckin door before we set the whole place on fire! I said, open the door!"

I could faintly hear Mom say, "We don't have any gold. I can't give you what we don't have. Please just leave us alone. You've already killed my husband, what more do you want?"

"We want our gold. Open this fuckin door, do it now."

Oh no! I thought I heard one of the bars being lifted from the door and I knew I had to react immediately, or Mom and our baby were going to be killed too. I walked slowly towards the cabin with my pistol in hand but behind my back. The one called Jimmy, turned and saw me. He smiled and said, "My god, you've grown nearly into womanhood. Dickey look at this. She is so pretty. Your name is, whatchamacallit, Fanny or is it Annie? Makes me no never mind, get over here and say hello."

I walked towards them and noticed the big grins on both their faces. Jimmy stared at my chest and then at my legs. He said, "Come over here and give Uncle Jimmy a hug."

I did as he asked. I walked towards him and when I got within about three feet, I brought my gun around and shot him twice in the stomach. He dropped to the ground. I then turned to face Dickey and as I did, I felt something strike the left side of my forehead. It burned me and stunned me. I quickly fired a shot at him, and I think it hit his left arm. I felt another shot go into my side, as I fired another shot at Dickey's midsection, and then I inadvertently dropped my pistol. Dickey had dropped to the ground, but not before he fired another shot that grazed my thigh. I limped over and picked up his gun that he had dropped on the ground close to him and I pointed it at his face. I said, "You killed my dog and my Dad, and you shot me. You were also going to kill my Mom and my little sister. All this for some gold we don't have. Why?"

Dickey was dying, but he wanted to tell me something, maybe to clear his conscience, "Your daddy was a very bad man. He robbed us six months ago. He killed two of my friends and wounded another. He stole all the gold we had panned from that damn creek and ran away with it. That holster you got on was my friend Stevie's, his mama put the beading on it for him. There is gold around here somewhere and that thief Crow stole it from us. And this place? How do you think Crow got this cabin and barn? He killed Davy, Lenny and Phil to get it. Did you think that lazy Injun built this all by himself? Davy befriended him and what did he get for all his trouble, a shot in the head?" Dickey began choking and breathing hard. He finally passed on without saying another word.

I yelled, "Mom, I've been shot please help me, it's okay, you can come out now."

Mom removed the wooden bolts from the door and came running out and looked over her dead husband and cried. She sat down on the ground besides me and asked, "Where are you shot. I can see your forehead but where else?"

I replied, "Here on my side near my stomach and my leg. Mom, I hurt so much, am I going to die?"

"You are not going to die. I won't let that happen. Let me get you inside and I'll look you over."

Mom had me lay on the floor at first, before she re-bolted the door. She was afraid there were more of these men that wanted Dad's gold or our bodies. She took off my top and bottoms and quietly said, "Sweetie, it's bad, but it could be worse. I need to stop the bleeding and it will be painful. Let me help you up and I'll get you onto your bed. I'll need to cauterize the wounds on your leg and your side. This will hurt like hell, but it has to be done. You've already lost so much blood; I have to do this right now."

I remember Mom taking that poker we use in the fireplace and getting it red hot. She then came over to me with the poker in her hand and said, "Annie, this is going to hurt me more than you, please forgive me." That's the last thing I remembered from that day. I will say this, '*That was the most painful three seconds of my life.*'

I woke two days later with Mom sitting beside me on the bed. She smiled and said, "You are still the prettiest girl I've ever seen. How are you feeling?"

I said, "I'm not sure yet. I hurt all over but not as bad when you put that poker on my side. Has the bleeding stopped?"

"Yes, the bleeding has stopped. I sewed up the wound on your head the best I could, I'm sure there be a scar, but it won't be too noticeable. Now, the other scars will be more noticeable, but they're on your body where just you and maybe your future husband can enjoy them together."

Mom laughed at her comments as I did too. She is so sweet. I replied, "Mom, what about Dad's body? And what are you going to do with the bodies of the men I killed?"

She was very stoic and said, "I think Dad was the bad man and maybe not the men you had to kill. I buried Dad over by the stands of trees by the barn. I dragged the dead men into the forest using one of the ponies. I left them far away from our home, a place where no one will find the bodies, or I should say bones. I did find the stash of gold that Dad stole. It was in the barn, in the farthest corner from the entryway. After looking around for an hour or so, I found a spot where he had piled some dirt over about ten logs that were nicely tucked together. Annie, below the logs was his stash, I lifted up the logs and there it was. There is a fortune in gold but also silver. Dad must have been robbing and killing miners for a very long time. Annie, there is so much gold, I don't know what to do with all of it. I brought it all in the cabin and put it in the escape hatch. Can you rest now, and we'll talk more about this later, when you're feeling better. Okay?"

As I was falling back to sleep, I muttered, "Yeah Mom, we'll talk later."

CHAPTER SIXTEEN

The Truth About Crow

I was in constant pain for at least three weeks. After that things got slowly better. Mom watched me like a hawk, she wouldn't let me out of her sight. But she also watched little Addie-Lou like that too. She was afraid some more bad men would come looking for Dad. What was wrong with him? Why did he kill and steal from the miners? Maybe it was retribution for them killing his wife and little daughter. Stealing their gold is one thing but killing them is completely different. Go figure. I guess you never can understand why people do the things they do. Dad was so nice to me, Mom and Addie-Lou, it was hard to see him killing people just for their gold.

As the days passed, I got stronger and had less pain. Mom was very attentive to me and I liked it. After Addie-Lou was born most of Mom's attention was centered on her, and rightly so. But I know Mom and I loved one another, and we'd be together as a family for a very long time. But I needed to explain some things to her about dear old Dad.

After putting Addie-Lou down for her nap, Mom and I walked outside to talk. I began, "Mom, I don't think you know just how bad Crow was. I found another stash in the barn the other day and it was hidden in that old wagon and it wasn't gold or silver. It was revolvers, rifles and ammo. So many I couldn't count them all. Also, swords and knives. Dad and I were accosted by a couple of rogues a long while back and they wanted me. He killed them immediately. He then told me that is how he accumulated all of his weapons. I never thought for one minute there would be so many. Mom he must have killed many men to accumulate all of the weapons in that wagon. Come with me and I'll show you."

Mom said, "You think he may have killed more men than we originally thought? Just for gold and guns? My goodness he was a madman. Annie, do you think he could have snapped one day and killed us?"

I nodded my head yes and said, "I think he may have killed his wife and daughter too. I don't know for sure, but he may have. Mom, I need to tell you something else. When that man Dickey was dying, he asked me if I knew how Dad got this cabin and barn. I didn't answer him because I thought he might be trying to deceive me to get the upper hand. That wasn't the case at all. Later after he died, I guessed he was trying to clear his conscience. But he said that Dad had killed Davy, Phil and Lenny to get this cabin and barn. He said, 'Did you think your Dad built all of this by himself?' Mom, did Crow ever tell you how he got this cabin and barn?"

"When I first saw this place, I asked him if he built all of this by himself and if so, how long did it take? I said it must have taken years in the making. He replied that he cleared all the land and built the cabin and barn by himself. He said it took him only two years."

"Mom, think about it. Clearing the land by himself would take longer than two years. Then he'd have to cut all the trees and find a way to stack all the logs for the cabin and the barn. No man could have done that by himself. I never asked him about it, I had just guessed he found it abandoned and fixed it up."

"Annie, I'm certain he told me he did all the work himself. What did we get ourselves into? My guess there will be more men showing up looking for him. Do you think we should leave here?"

"Mom, he killed men that were his friends. They helped him find the men that killed his mom. His friends! They built this place and he killed them so he could have it. But no, we shouldn't leave, this is our home. I do think we should take advantage of all the weapons and ammo I found in that old wagon. First, we should both get more acquainted with all those weapons and learn to shoot them. Second, I am also going to learn to quick draw Dad's Colt revolver. Third, we are never going to be without a gun when we go out of the house. And last, but not least, if an animal or human knocks, scratches or tries to enter this house the door and window will remain closed and bolted. If they attempt to burn the place down, we'll hide in the escape hatch."

Mom was smiling. She laughingly said, "Yes Sir, we'll do exactly what you recommended, Sir." Mom was now laughing hysterically. She must have thought my diatribe was really funny. At first, I was offended, but a second later I saw the humor in all of it. I laughed too. In fact, we both were laughing so hard we woke up little Addie-Lou. Mom hugged me and said, "My goodness, I can't believe how much I love you. God blessed me when you came into my life. Crow did two good things in this life; he gave me you and Addie-Lou."

Both Mom and I began our daily ritual of target practicing and I also practiced my quick drawing. And I must say I was getting damn good. But practicing quick draw and shooting at a target is much easier than shooting at a human. But I have done that too, so I feel I'm prepared for anything.

Something else happened to me as I turned fifteen years old; I became a woman. Mom had explained what to expect and said it was the woman's curse. I never experienced that type of discomfort before and keep in mind I've been shot three times. Mom said it would get better and it did.

CHAPTER SEVENTEEN

WILD WIND

It is now 1873 and the civil war has been over for about seven or eight years. During the latter part of the war, many rebels in the confederacy deserted and headed for the wild west. They came this way to pan for gold and find a better life. The population of the west was increasing by leaps and bounds. It would be ten long years before the railroads would make it into Montana, and the horse and wagons were still the best mode of travel.

Mom, Addie-Lou and I were happy living alone on top of our hill in the wild. We hadn't had any visitors since Crow died but we were always on the lookout for trouble. I was the hunter for our family and deer meat was our main choice of food. Mom tended to the gardens, but I also helped her with that. Addie-Lou was now four years old and getting big and she was so much fun. Mom and I loved her so.

It was early fall when he came into our homestead. He was a young Indian brave, and he was riding a painted pony. He wore the traditional Indian garb, buckskin pants, shirt and moccasins on his feet. He didn't have any weapons that I could visibly see. I was walking towards the cabin when I first saw him. He smiled at me and said, "Hello, I mean you no harm. My name is Wild Wind, and I am of the Cheyenne Nation. Please don't be afraid."

I replied as I pointed my Winchester rifle at him, "I'm not afraid. You are the one that should be afraid. I do mean to harm you if I have to. What do you want?"

"What is your name? Please put that rifle down, I told you I mean you no harm."

Just then Mom came out of the cabin and pointed her Winchester rifle at him too. She said, "What do you want? How did you find us? What do you want? Who else is with you?"

The man said, "I want nothing, and I am alone. I saw the smoke from your chimney and rode up to investigate. I heard there were two women living alone somewhere in this direction. I came to warn you that some bad men are heading this way."

I said, "Why would an Indian warn us of coming danger? What are you expecting to get out of all this?"

"I expect nothing. A woman that I am close to in my tribe asked me to warn you about the danger. Her name is Manda and she is my grandmother. Some fur traders came into our camp to trade for furs. They asked if anyone in our tribe knew Crow's whereabouts. One brave said he thought he knew where he lived and told the traders the directions to where he thought they might find Crow. The traders did not say why they wanted that information, but Manda knew others were looking for Crow too."

I asked, "So, Manda told you to warn us? That was really nice of her, so very nice of her. She's your grandmother? How long do you think it will be before they get here?"

"My name, as I said before is Wild Wind, please call me Wind. My guess is it will take them a few days to get here. Their wagons are full of furs and that will slow them down. I'm here to help you."

I looked him over and he was not handsome but not bad looking. He did have some of the Indian features, but his skin was almost as white as mine. I asked him, "How much of you is Indian? You look almost white."

Wind replied, “My mother as well as my grandmother are both white, and my father was a half-breed. My mother is dead, she died in childbirth a few years ago. She had the baby, but it also died. My father died a several months ago. There is something in the air that’s killing many Indians and it killed my father. They called it smallpox, diphtheria or something like that. The chief’s think it’s the white man trying to kill us off someway. The tribe is so poor now, with the buffalo herds being depleted because of the white man and the supposed lack of demand for their fur. It’s funny to me that the traders still want to barter for those buffalo hides when they say there is little demand for them.”

I said, “Why are the traders coming here? Don’t they know Crow is dead?”

Wind shook his head and said, “Crow is dead? I did not know that. When and how did that happen?”

Mom replied, “It happened a while ago. Some men had been looking for him and they found him and killed him. My daughter Annie here, killed them but was wounded herself. She has just healed from her gunshot wounds in the last couple of months. There were others looking for him too and Annie also took care of them. We didn’t know it, but Crow was not a good man. He killed many miners for their gold and weapons. I won’t go into any more details than that.”

Wind looked at me and said, “You have a grizzly claw hanging from your neck. What does that represent? In the Indian world a man cannot wear that unless he killed the bear. Are you aware of that?”

“Yes, I’m aware of that. My mother here made a full necklace with the other claws but left one for this necklace until I get older and bigger.”

“So, you did kill a grizzly? If so, I’m very impressed. Not only are you a hunter but you are a beautiful one at that.”

I was so embarrassed by those comments, I couldn't speak. I'm sure my face turned bright red. Mom saved the day, she said, "Wind you are right, my daughter is a great hunter and she did kill a grizzly bear by herself. She has also been the protector of me and my other daughter Addie-Lou. And you are also right; she is a very beautiful, smart young woman. Now, we'll need to get ready for the trappers."

I looked Wind over and I got chills running down my back. Wow, this is a really nice feeling. I was finally able to say, "Are you planning on helping us?"

Wind said, "I assure you I'm here to help but I'm uncertain what I'll be able to do. I'm not very good with any weapons. By the way, my Cheyenne name is Minninnewah, meaning Wild Wind."

I responded, "I'll just call you Wind, I like that better than Minninny, or whatever you called yourself."

Wind replied, "Whatever you'd like, Annie, whatever you'd like. Just let me stay here and help you and your family out as much as I can."

CHAPTER EIGHTEEN

FRIENDSHIP?

We knew we were in for trouble and it would be coming soon. Mom asked for my advice on what we should do to protect ourselves. I suggested we move out of the cabin and into the woods until we were attacked. I also liked the idea of finding the trappers before they found us. Wind agreed with me, he thought we'd be better off taking them on away from our home, in other words Indian style, surprise the hell out of them.

I asked Wind if he would like to join me in trying to locate the trappers. And he replied in a very eager tone, "Why yes, I would like to travel with you. I think we could find them in just a day or two and we could sneak up on them. Surprise attack is the Indian way and as you know I'm part Indian."

I smiled at him and said, "So you wouldn't mind traveling with a woman? And you don't think I'd be a detriment in a gunfight?"

"No, I think if anything, you will be better than me in a gunfight. It appears you've killed your share of bad men and to be honest with you, I've never killed anyone. And I've never killed a grizzly or a black bear for that matter. I'm a virgin in all those matters."

I was laughing very hard when I said, "A virgin in all those matters? A virgin? You could have used a better term than that, like inexperienced."

Wind wasn't laughing but Mom sure was. I then asked, "How did you learn to speak such good English?"

Wind quietly said "My mother taught me, and she and my father always spoke English around me when we were alone. They felt with all the white men flooding the territory, English was going to be the language that would be most used in the future. Cheyenne would probably be the least used."

I said, "Alright Mr. Virgin let's make a plan." I laughed pretty hard at my comment, but I realized that Wind and my mom weren't laughing now. They were both very quiet.

Wind had an angry look on his face. I thought he was about to yell at me, but before he did, he quickly took a deep breathe, stopped and composed himself. He quietly said, "Please call me Wind and nothing else. I realized that you look upon me as someone that is weak and not qualified to help you. You are likely correct. If you'd like me to leave, I'd be happy to do so. I know you're trying to be funny at my expense, but I've had enough of that to last me a lifetime. I thought you might be different, but you are not."

I was stunned by his comments, I said, "What in the hell brought that on? I was just teasing you. I'm sorry if I offend you. It won't happen again; believe me it won't ever happen again. If you want to leave, do it and don't come back."

Mom was stunned by what I had just said, "Annie, you owe Wind an apology. And Wind, I'm sorry I laughed at that virgin comment, I should not have done that. Clearly you have some deep-rooted issues about being teased."

Wind just turned and walked to his horse and mounted him and road away. I was perplexed and offended. I said to Mom, "What just happened here? I was just teasing. Why did he leave us? I was just teasing"

Mom said, "I'm sorry Annie, I could tell right away you kind of liked him. I believe he's led a life of being ridiculed by the tribe members, especially by the younger braves. As he said, his mother was white, and his dad was a mix of Indian and white. That doesn't usually bode well for young braves. Think about what Crow went through having a white mother. Those Indians can be brutal."

"Oh Mom, I'm so sorry. Boy did I screw this up. We needed his help and now he's gone."

"I don't think he went too far away. I think he really liked you."

I was feeling really down after Wind left. I guess I didn't realize that boys sometimes went through the same thing us girls go through having older brothers. I was the brunt of all the jokes in my family and only my mom tried to protect me."

I was walking back to the barn area when Wind rode back into our yard. He jumped off his pony and said, "They're about half a day's ride away. I saw them while I was riding down the hill. They are moving very slowly. Their wagon must be full. I suspect they will stop for the night and try and attack us tomorrow morning."

I walked over to him and said, "Thanks for coming back, are you planning on helping us? We could really use your help. And I am so sorry about what I said, I promise I will never do that ever again. Please forgive me."

Wind stared at me before saying, "You are so beautiful. You're even more beautiful when you are feeling guilty about something. I wasn't leaving when I left here before, I was going to try and find them. So, should we watch from the hill today and see if they stop for the night and then try and attack?"

I was smiling ear to ear and said, "Yes, that's a good idea. We'll sit somewhere on the hill and watch. If they stop, we'll go and confront them. I'll go tell Mom what's happening. She and Addie-Lou should stay locked up in the cabin until it's all over."

After I told Mom of our plan, Wind and I rode down the hill and found a nice place to watch for the wagons. We hid the horses behind some boulders and sat down in the middle of a stand of trees. We sat very close to one another and it felt really nice to be sitting next to someone you kind of liked.

As we sat and watched I asked Wind, "Please don't take this the wrong way but I'd like to ask you a very personal question."

Wind said, "Ask away."

"All right then, have you ever kissed a girl? I mean a girl you liked?"

He smiled and said, "No I haven't. Have you ever kissed a boy you liked?"

"No, I haven't but I like you and would I like to kiss you."

Wind slid over and kissed me on the lips. That kiss lasted a long time, for neither of us wanted it to stop. I was finally able to slide away and say, "Wow, that was so nice. Would you mind if we did that again, maybe a lot of times again?"

After way too many kisses I said, "I think we should stop now. I'm feeling some things I've never experienced before. You know physically?"

Wind replied, "I think I know what you mean. However, I felt those things many times before but when I was alone. I do know another thing though; I really like you."

"I kind of feel the same way. But we should be watching for the traders."

Wind stood up and looked out on the prairie and he spotted the wagons coming our way. He said, "Annie, I'm sure they'll spend the night on the prairie, just look where they are. They're still several miles away just before dark. We'll attack after they get asleep. Whaddya think?"

"You're the boss, we do as you say." I smiled at him after I said that, and he smiled right back.

We held hands and hugged each other as for a long time. Wind finally said, "We should get going. We'll need to tether the horses and walk a mile or so and wait for them to fall asleep. We have the Winchesters and we both have a six-shooter."

CHAPTER NINETEEN

ANDY

Wind and I waited until the trappers had drank themselves silly and passed out before we walked the mile or so to their campsite. They had been loud, so loud that their voices had permeated over the entire prairie. We heard them talking about all the fun they'd have killing Crow and having sex with his women. They'd have sex slaves for the rest of their lives. They sounded so drunk and so happy, except one of them. He told them that it wasn't right to take women against their will. After he had said that we heard a loud slap and a voice say, "Yous shut that hole in yous face! No one's asked yous about yous opinion. Wees didn't plan on sharing the women with yous anyway, yous too damn young. And, since yous likes Crow so much, we'll just have yous be the one that slits his Injun throat. How'd ya like that?"

However, the other person retorted, "I'll not be killing anyone, and I won't force myself on any woman now or when I get older, that's for sure. Crow never did nothing to me. I liked him, even though he was a thief."

Another slap permeated across the prairie. The voice said, "Don't yous ever talk like that again. Wees saved yous ass from dem damn Injun's and yous will dos as we say, understand? Yous done been eaten our food and drunk our water, so yous will do as wee's say or yous will starve to death. It don't mean no never mind to wees if yous die. Yous are what wees called in the old days an 'indentured servant.' Yous owes us for us trading dem damn blankets to dem damn Injun's for yous ass."

After that exchange, the camp became very quiet. We began our walk towards their camp then. Wind quietly asked, "That sounded like a young kid didn't it?"

I whispered, "Yes it did. I'm guessing he was taken from his home or from a wagon train by the Indians and sold to these assholes. Please forgive my bad language, but that's what they are, assholes."

Wind was smiling ear to ear, he quietly said, "I think we both know what it's like to be controlled by bad men and the tribes. As I said, my mom was a white woman, and my dad was a half breed. Dad had it easier than my ma. He was really a good man and took very good care of us. He was made to go to war against the white man and also on the other tribes. That was his demise. We never even got to see his body, they just left it on the prairie to rot. Since he was part white man, he didn't get the tradition Indian burial."

"Wind, why didn't you go to war and how did you get away?"

"I refused to kill another man, so I was belittled by the tribe and was made to stay with the women. I was an outcast in the tribe. Everyone made fun of me and belittled me. They called me a little girl, a little white girl at that. My mom and dad tried in vain to protect me but weren't able to do so. I was beaten by the young braves and by many of the older ones too. Manda gave me my chance to get away, that's how I got here. And Annie, I'm so happy to be here with you. I'm also going to show you today that I'm not a coward."

I had tears in my eyes, and they were slowly running down my face after Wind told me about his life in the tribe. I stopped and hugged him and pressed my body close to his. Wow, did that feel good!

We walked until we heard the drunken trappers snoring. Boy, were they loaded. It must have been the shine they drank. We first cut the leather rope on their tethered horses and let them walk away. No one stirred. We then walked close to where they were lying and a voice said, "Don't worry, they won't wake up, they're too drunk to wake up. Hi, I'm Andy, are you friends of Crow?"

Wind and I looked at each other with confused looks on our faces. I said, "Yes, I'm Crow's daughter Annie and this here is Wind."

"It's nice to meet you all. What are your plans? Are you gonna kill um? They deserve killing. They are very bad men."

I replied, "First off, how old are you?"

Andy answered, "I'm ten. I was taken I think about a year ago. They took me to use as trade bait, but no one wanted me until these men came along. The Indians killed my mom and dad. My mom was really nice, but my dad was a terrible man. The only people that have beat me more than him is these assholes."

Wind and I began to laugh but quickly stopped when one of the traders began to stir in his blanket. I said, "We'll tell you later why we we're laughing. I guess we should wake up these assholes."

Andy quietly said, "I'll get their guns first." Andy walked around the three men and took their guns from their holsters. They also had three antiquated rifles leaning against one of the wagons. Andy put them into the back wagon out of sight from the traders.

I yelled, "It's wake up time boys, it's wake up time! Everyone up." I walked over to where they were lying, and I kicked two of them in their butts. Again, I yelled, "That means you asshole and your pimple face friend. And look at this one Wind, have you ever seen a dirtier excuse for a man than him?"

The man that had slapped Andy was clearly the leader, he said, "What the hell is the meaning of this? Wees are fur traders and trappers, nuttin more, nuttin less. Explain yourself woman?" He then began to look for his six-shooter.

Andy laughed at the man and said, "Harvey, here's your gun, it's right here. You don't look so tough right now, what's wrong? Did you let this little woman here get the drop on you and your boys? I bet you won't be able to talk your way out of this jam. You know they heard everything you said tonight."

Harvey was not going to give into a woman, or an Indian or this young boy. He stumbled to his feet and tried to grab Andy. I immediately hit him on the head with the butt-end my Winchester. He fell to the ground screaming and crying. He yelled, "What in the hell be wrong with yous woman? I's a defenseless man here, yous done hurt me bad. Yous should be home cooking and taking care of a man, not out here trying to prove you're as good as a man."

I looked him over and he was as dirty as the others. I thought, *'they were intent on making Mom and me their sex slaves. I couldn't even imagine how awful that would have been. I also laughed to myself about his comment about cooking and taking care of a man.'* I finally said, "Mr. Harvey, sir, I'm so sorry I hit you, I didn't mean to hurt you. I just didn't want you to harm young Andy here again. What can I do to make you feel better? How about sex? Would you like to have sex with me now?"

Harvey looked bewildered; I think my comments about having sex confused him. He didn't know what to say. The other two assholes did, however. The one call Harry said, "Yeah and when he's done wit ya, I'm next."

I listened to what intelligent Harry had to say and then walked over to where he was sitting, and I hit him with the butt-end of my Winchester too. He dropped over with a thud, like a rotten apple dropping from a tree. Harry was bleeding profusely from the top of his bald head. I looked at the one called Frank and he was crying so hard he stuttered out, "You hurt my brother, you fuckin bitch, I'll kill ya! I'll kill ya!"

I turned toward Frank and I fired a round that skinned the top of his head. He dropped to the ground screaming, "I'm sorry, I'm so sorry, please forgive me. I'll do whatever you ask."

Wind came over by me and said, "Andy just told me that these boys intentionally traded contaminated blankets and clothing to the Indians for these furs. The tribe must be suffering so. What if we were to take them back to the tribe and let them deal with them? I think the whole Cheyenne nation would be indebted to us."

"I'd like that. Just maybe they'd let us move around the prairie about with any confrontations. Let's do it. But first, I'll need to tell my mom what we're doing. We'll leave Andy with her and Addie-Lou."

Wind said, "Take Andy with you and tell your mom where we're headed. I'll watch these assholes. Hurry back, the quicker we get back to the tribe the more lives we'll save."

CHAPTER TWENTY

Return to The Cheyenne Camp

Wind had tied all the trader's hands behind their backs with the leather rope we took off the tethered horses. He made sure the ropes were tight and he could tell they were tight by all the whining and complaining he was hearing from the traders. He took the rifles out of the last wagon and unloaded them. He then forced all the traders in the back of the wagon. He then tied their feet together also with the leather rope. He sat and waited for me to return.

I got back to the cabin within two hours and knocked hard on the door, and yelled, "Mom, it's me, Annie. I've got a new friend for you, and some furs, hurry now and open up."

I heard the wooden bolts being lifted and heard Mom say, "I'm hurrying, is everything alright? Did you find the men that were looking for Crow?"

"Yes, we did." Mom came out and smiled at Andy. I said, "Mom, this is Andy. He thinks he's around ten years old and he is going to stay with us. He was taken by the Cheyenne and sold to the traders. He can sleep in my bed until I get home. We are going to take the traders and one of their wagons back to the Cheyenne so they can make them suffer. They traded contaminated blankets and clothing to them and who knows how many have died. We should be back in a couple of weeks; Wind is coming with me. Also, there is a wagon full of buffalo hides outside, please put the wagon and the hides in the barn. We'll decide what to do with them when I get back."

Mom smiled and said, "Just be careful, I don't want any grandchildren just yet. I know you two like one another."

I said, "Mom, it's not like that. But he's really nice." I then left them and was on my way to meet Wind, for our new travel experiences together.

When I got back Wind was raring to go. He had the trappers or traders, I didn't know what to call them, tied up and sitting in the wagon. I said, "Looks like you're ready, so am I. You do know we haven't slept yet. How about us moving out for a while and then one of us will sleep while the other guards them. You sleep first when we stop. I'm wound too tight; I always have a hard time sleeping when I'm excited."

Wind said, "Let's ride until daybreak and then I'll sleep. We'll also stop late afternoon, and you'll sleep. We both will ride at night. That way we can keep these assholes from trying to take us at night."

We rode until around five o'clock the next morning. Wind slept for a couple of hours and then we were off again. The traders begged and pleaded with us to let them go, they claimed they had done nothing wrong. Their pleas fell on deaf ears. I reminded them they had likely killed many women and children along with many braves. They countered my reminder by saying all them damn Injuns deserved to die. I couldn't believe that these men could take a human's life so nonchalantly. I could hardly wait to see their reaction when we got back to the Cheyenne camp.

It took us almost four days to finally arrive near the Cheyenne encampment. We were met by a war party that was very serious about stopping us. They came at us whopping and hollering with their bows and arrows in their hands. Wind stood up on the wagon seat and screamed something at them. I was sure that would stop them. It didn't, they surrounded us with bows drawn. Wind was attempting to explain to them why we were here, but they wouldn't listen. One of the braves grabbed me by my arm and dragged me off my horse. I fell to the ground very hard and I almost passed out. Wind jumped off the wagon and stopped immediately. I think he may have been afraid of the consequences. I however, jumped up before he could get to me, with my six-shooter drawn and I shoved it under the jaw of the Indian that pulled me off my horse. I cocked the hammer and stared at him before I cracked him on the side of his head with the butt end of my gun. He dropped to the ground in pain. Wind was now shouting louder than ever, and I think they were finally listening to him. All of a sudden it became very quiet. Wind said, "Annie, will you please get into the back of the wagon with me? These braves say they will take us to their camp."

We were then forced into the back of the wagon with the traders. Harvey laughed at us and said, "Looks like yous will be getting a man now, maybe many more now. I's hope they screw ya to death."

We entered the Cheyenne camp two hours later and saw what was left of the tribe. I guessed that about half the tribe had died. What was left came out to see what the war party had brought home. Well, I wouldn't say they were happy to see us, I'd say they might be happy to kill us. They were very angry and when they saw the traders, they got very riled up. It was then I saw Manda walking closer to the wagon. She asked, "Wind, what is going on here and who is this young woman?"

Wind replied, "Manda, these are the traders that traded the contaminated blankets and clothing to the tribe a few weeks ago. We found them before they could attack us. This is Annie, Crows daughter."

Manda smiled at me and said, "Please say nothing right now, I will try and calm everyone down."

After Manda explained why we were there, they all began talking to one another.

I said to Manda, "If I were you folks, I'd burn all the blankets and clothing these men left you with. Those things must be carrying the disease."

Manda smiled at me and said, "It's nice to see you again Annie, you've grown into a beautiful young woman. I heard what you did to one of our braves. He'll have a hard time living that down. And the blankets and clothing have already been burned. We figured it was the blankets immediately after people began to die. But thank you for bringing these men back to us so we can settle the score. You'll not want to see what is going to happen to them."

I replied, "I'd rather not see or hear what is going to happen to them. But about that brave, some men have a hard time realizing that women can be strong. That brave thought I was going to sit and cry after he pulled me off my horse. I guess I surprised him."

Manda smiled and said, "Did you think I'd ever forget you? I remember you so well, the way you handled the Nose. She died from the knife wound shortly after you left with Crow. You were a tough little cookie then and you still are now. I'm glad our brave saw firsthand how a woman can react when being pushed around. I'm sure you would have killed him under different circumstances. I know I would have and I'm not nearly as tough as you are."

"Thanks for the compliment. One thing I would like you to ask the elders is; if we were to go into tribal lands in the future would they please leave us alone? I'd like them to know we didn't need to bring these trappers back here, we thought you'd need to know about the blankets."

"Annie, the elders have told me that they have already ordered everyone in the tribe, including the brave you hit, to let you pass everywhere in our country. You have their word. They appreciate you bringing these bad men back here. On another note, do you know what happened to a young boy named Andy? The tribe sold him to these men, and he left with them. He was such a nice boy."

I smiled and said, "He is with my mother and my little sister Addie-Lou. I'm sure he'll be staying with us. I'm also hoping Wind will come back with me, I kind of like him."

"Wild Wind is a very nice person. He's my grandson. I think he'd do better with your family than with us. I'm going to encourage him to go with you. First, I must tell him about some of the deaths that have happened since he left. And I understand Crow was killed. Did he treat you well?"

I replied, "Yes, he did. He also treated my mother Sue Stands-Alone very well too, as well as my little sister Addie-Lou. He did, however, kill and steal from others. As time has gone by, several men have come looking for him. One of them killed him in front of Mom and me. I killed the man that did the killing. I've heard Dad was not a good man."

Manda took a deep breath before saying, "You're correct, he was not a good man. I'm not sure what happened to his wife and child. There were rumors floating around that he thought his wife had a lover. Someone found his wife's dead body, along with his little girls near a stand of trees close to the town of Settler Gulch with bullet wounds to their heads. A strange man's body was lying next to them. His head was decapitated from his body. No one knew who the man was. Someone told Crow about his family so he could bury them. But the bodies were never buried, they were just left there to rot. Now that's the rumor that I heard."

I just shook my head, and said, "What was wrong with him? Both Mom and I thought he was capable of hurting us after we had heard what he had done to the miners. But he never showed us any of that anger. I'd like to just forget all the things I heard about him. Thanks for telling me that Manda."

After Manda had explained to Wind about all the deaths, he came looking for me. When he found me by the wagon he said, "Manda said you might be alright with me coming along with you back home. Would you be?"

I replied, "Yes, that would be fine, but I want you to know I'm too young to be married. I like you, but I don't know what love is all about. I have to watch over my mom and sister and now Andy too. So, if you want to come along as my friend, I'd like that."

"I'm fine with that Annie."

CHAPTER TWENTY-ONE

LOVE/SEX??

We left the Cheyenne encampment and headed home. We took our time, and I had a wonderful time with Wind. We hugged and kissed and the more we did that, the more confused I got. Love? What the hell is love? I have so many mixed feelings about all this stuff. I liked it when Wind touched me all over and I could tell he liked it when I did it to him. But I know the result of going any further is having what Mom called intercourse. She has also called it fucking, but she also told me not to use that word; it is not ladylike. Now that I think about the word 'fucking', Mom says that all the time. I never hear her say, 'I hate this damn intercourse of a house.' No, it's always, 'I hate this damn fucking house.' I look at my mom as very ladylike. She is polite, kind and beautiful in every way, but she does say the word fuck every once in a while, when she gets mad. I will still try and not use that word, however, if I do use it by mistake, I will not worry that I'm not a lady. But I do know one thing, I will not be having intercourse or fucking anytime soon in my life. I don't want a baby now, or maybe ever. Taking care of Addie-Lou has been hard enough for me. I love that little kid, but I don't want any more of them.

Wind has not pressed me to do anything more than what we are doing. He's as inexperienced as I am, maybe more. I don't think his mom or dad told him anything about where babies come from. I did, so I have more experience than he does. I feel very proud of that.

We arrived home after a week of slow travel. When we rode up our hill Mom came out to greet us. Andy came along and he was holding Addie-Lou. After we dismounted, Andy handed Addie-Lou to me. She was all smiles and giggles. She is so cute. Maybe I'll have just one baby. Only one.

Andy followed me around like a little puppy. I like him and he's fun to be around. He's very inquisitive and asks questions about everything. However, when I ask him questions about his family he clams up. He just pretends he doesn't hear me. I notice that he stays clear of Wind. I don't think he's ever uttered a single word to him. I'm beginning to think it's the Indian clothing Wind wears. Maybe it's time for a change? I've always wanted to go to that little town called Settler Gulch that Crow spoke of. It's where he met Mom.

I asked Mom about the town and she said it wasn't worth visiting. And then I asked why? She said, "Well, the town as they call it, was originally called Dead Man's Gulch. The reason being, so many men died while panning for gold in the stream that runs through it. The stream was named River of Gold by the early miners that found a few big nuggets there. After that, the place was overrun with prospectors searching to hit it big. There were so few women when I was there, I was accosted every day by men wanting to pay me for sex."

I replied, "You said sex? Did you mean they wanted you for intercourse, or was it they wanted to fuck you?" At first, I giggled a bit and then it turned to laughter. I then looked at Mom and she was laughing too. It then turned into hysterical laughter by both of us. Addie-Lou, Andy and Wind came into the cabin and were asking what was so funny. That made Mom and me to laugh harder. Finally, Mom was hugging me and laughing. It then turned to tickling each other. It was one of the best times I ever had with my mom. She is so nice,

I'm so glad I have her, even if it's only for a short time longer. I'll get to more of that a little bit later.

So, after all the laughter I got serious. I said, "Mom, I want to take Wind and go into that hellhole they call something or other Gulch and try and get some clothes. Addie-Lou, Andy, Wind and I all need some clothes. I think Andy would be more inclined to talk to Wind if he didn't wear Indian garb. There is a trading post, isn't there?"

Mom replied, "Yes there is, but this trip could be dangerous. I refuse to go along with you. I am so fearful of going back there. You and Wind go ahead, but I warn you both now, be on your guard for trouble. I'll get you some silver coins from our hiding place, but never take any gold. If you do, they will follow you back here thinking there is gold in our little creek."

"Mom, you know I'll be careful, but you also know I can take care of myself. Wind and I will go to the barn and find some weapons to take along with us. We do have the Winchester's and Wind will need a handgun and holster."

Wind and I walked into the barn and headed for the cache of weapons we had stored in the old wagon. I said, "My goodness Wind, I didn't remember that we had so many weapons in here. Find a gun and holster you like; I'm going to look for a knife."

After an hour of going through and sorting all the weapons, Wind found a Colt revolver he liked. He also found a holster that fit the gun. I found the knife I had dreamed of ever since I had to gut that grizz. It was a very large knife; the blade was about ten inches long and about an inch and half wide. It had a large sheath that went along with it and it was sharp, very sharp. Wind smiled at me as he saw how excited I was. He said, "Do you know anything about that knife?"

I replied, "What do you mean? It's a knife, a very big, sharp knife and it's just what I always wanted."

Wind had a serious look on his face when he said, "That's a Bowie knife. The guy it was named after was Jim Bowie and he was man not to be trifled with. He wanted a big knife like you did and he had someone design and make a knife like you're holding right now. It was named for him after he killed someone in a knife fight duel. Now that's how the story goes. It is big medicine in the Indian culture. I've only seen one in my life and it was taken by our Chief from a prospector he killed. You hit the jackpot in finding that knife, it's worth a lot of gold."

"That's good to know, I won't show it off, I'll just wear it tucked into my boot."

CHAPTER TWENTY-TWO

ATTACK AT SETTLERS GULCH

Wind and I mounted our horses, and I grabbed the rope to our harnessed pack horse and headed in the direction of Settlers Gulch. We guessed that it would take us around two days to get there and we were in kind of a hurry. The weather this October was getting cold and sleeping outdoors at this time of year would be difficult. The nice part of it was, Wind and I cuddled together to keep warm. It was also nice to be able to kiss him whenever I wanted too.

It took us two long days to reach what I now call just the Gulch. The town was not at all the way Mom described it. Instead of the sod huts there were wooden buildings. Now, not too many wooden buildings, but some. There were still sod huts out by the River of Gold. In fact, there were many sod huts out there. I guessed it was clear, gold was being found by the number of miners there working claims.

I told Wind, "Let's get our clothing and get the hell outta here as soon as possible. I don't like the looks we're getting from these men. I also think you being dressed in Indian garb has riled some of them up."

We walked into what was now called Gorman's General Store. A very nice skinny man, with a full head of black curly hair, introduced himself to us and he said, "Howdy, and top of the morning to ya. My name is Mike Gorman and I own this establishment, what can I do for you?"

I said, "It's nice to meet you Mr. Gorman, I'm Annie Crow and this is my friend Wind. We need clothing for us and for members of our family. Please help Wind first, he needs to get out of the clothes he has on, I think there are some people that resent the fact that he is part Indian."

As Mr. Gorman showed Wind the men's clothing, I looked at the women's clothing. I liked the dresses, but I didn't know if that would be appropriate for a girl like me. I guess I didn't care, we have the money so why not splurge? I also found two pairs of dungarees, a pair of boots and stockings as well. I also took three shirts and two pair of long johns. I took two dresses for Addie-Lou and two pairs of dungarees. Andy also needed clothes, so I bought him dungarees, shirts and long johns. I also found a small coat for Addie-Lou but didn't buy a coat for me or Andy. Mom was busy making coats for all of us from our horde of fur that was in the barn.

I put the clothing on the counter as Wind came out from the back room wearing his cowboy clothing. He had on dungarees, a gray shirt and a cowboy hat. He looked really cute, but I told he looked real handsome. I didn't want to embarrass him in front of Mr. Gorman, I'd do that later when we are alone. Mr. Gorman smiled when he told me what we owed. I think he may have feared we didn't have enough to pay for all of this. As I was paying our bill, Wind walked out of the store with all of our clothing. As he was putting our goods into the panniers on our pack horse, three men approached him. One of the men said, "Lookie here boys, we gots us an Injun pretending to be a white cowboy. That shit ain't gonna fly around here boy. Whatcha putting in those panniers?"

Wind was scared out of his mind. He said, "I'm a white man. My daddy was a half breed, and my mama was white. I'm just putting clothing for my family in these here panniers. I don't want no trouble."

I could hear from inside the store what was going on outside. I walked out of the store and stepped on to the ground and they all stopped harassing Wind and looked my way. One of the men walked closer to me and looked me up and down. He smiled and said, "Now ain't ya a real cutie? And look at those nice little titties. I think you need a real man, not this little pretend cowboy. Come over here darlyn, I's got something for ya."

I looked at this dirty old man and made up my mind; if had to kill this old fart and his friends I'd do it. I just wanted Wind to stay clear of all this. I looked at Wind and said, "Please get behind me, I think I can handle this." He did as he was told.

I then walked to the right of the three of them, closer to where the dirty old man was standing. I walked within a foot of him and said, "Did you say you had something for me. Well, I have something for you." I did a quick draw with my Colt revolver and shoved it under his jaw and said, "Do you want to die old man? Keep on talking then."

The old fart quickly reached up and grabbed the barrel of my Colt and turned it way from his throat and smiled at me. He said, "Whatcha gonna do now, you little bitch?" What he didn't know was, I had my new Bowie knife in my other hand.

I quietly said, "This!" I shoved the knife directly into his crotch area and twisted it very hard. The look on his face went from surprise, to execrating pain. He dropped to the ground screaming in pain. He was yelling, "She cut off my balls, she cut off my balls!"

I then turned to the two other men and pointed my Colt at them. They both raised their hands in a surrendering manner while one of them said, "We don't want no more trouble, no ma'am, we surely don't. Would you mind if we helped our old friend Russ out a bit?"

I looked them over and I didn't think they had the balls to fight me, if you get my meaning? I finally said, "I don't think your friend will be hassling any women again and I'm warning you two, if I see or hear that you're doing that shit again, I'll find you two and do the same to you as I did for your friend Russ here. I think you may want to help him, but if you don't, I'm sure he'll bleed to death. So long boys, I hope I see you all again." Before I mounted my horse, I looked around and saw that there was a large gathering of men watching what had happened. Not one said a word as Wind, and I mounted our horses and left the Gulch.

As we were riding away Wind said, "What in the world is wrong with you? Don't you think there was a better way to handle those men? My goodness woman, you cut off his balls and he'll likely bleed to death. There is no way to stop that type of bleeding."

I pulled on the reins on my horses and he stopped in his tracks. I shouted, "You fool! Did you think those nice men were going to let us walk away? You were not their target, I was! They wanted to rape me! And after the rape, who knows? They would have killed you, and do you want to know why? Because you're worthless to them, I'm not. They would have passed me around to all their friends and foes alike. It's called rape and then prostitution. They use women and sell their bodies to other men. Don't you ever talk to me again. When we get home, I want you out of my life for good. Do you understand?"

Wind was very apologetic, he said, "You're right, I didn't understand what they were going to do to you. I'm sorry for what I said, please forgive me. I'll leave you as soon as we get to your home."

"I don't want to talk to you. Stay clear of me, understand? You are the last person in the world that should judge me. All you damn Indians do is kill and rape white women. I saw it firsthand and I detest all of those Indian rapists. I vowed I'd never let a man rape me. Don't talk again or you'll end up like old Russ back there."

The ride home was long, cold and full of friction between Wind and me. I was sure he'd leave as soon as we got home. I didn't really care if he left us or not, but I did want him to understand why I did what I did. I felt I had no choice.

CHAPTER TWENTY-THREE

ROMANCE/WOLVES

When we got back to the cabin Mom knew right away something was not right. Addie-Lou has been walking for a long time now and she came running when I opened the door. She was all smiles. She wouldn't even look in Wind's direction, she wanted me to play with her. Andy was happy to see both of us. Mom said, "Since it's getting cold out, I'd like you two boys to sleep on the floor in the cabin. The barn will be too cold."

I quietly said, "Andy should sleep in the cabin, but Wind can stay in the barn." With a frown on my face I said, "I don't want Wind near me."

I turned and walked outside. I grabbed my Winchester and began to walk into the woods to hunt for a deer. After I had left Mom asked Wind what happened. He replied, "We had some trouble in the Gulch and Annie hurt one of the bad men that wanted her for sex, I think. She hurt him really bad, he'll likely die from the knife wound she gave him. I shouldn't have said anything, but I did. I said she could have handled it differently. She got very mad at me and told me off. She said she wanted me out of her home. I'm going to stay a couple of days and then I'm leaving. I don't know where I'll go but I can't stay here."

Mom said, "Wind, our Annie has a temper. But were those men going to try and rape her? She hates the thought of that happening to her and will do everything possible to hurt those types of men that would try and do that. I pity the poor bastard that ever tries anything like that on her again. I don't doubt that the assailant will die from his injuries. She wouldn't want them coming after her again in the future. Nor would I. Sometimes those types of men need to die. I have no feelings for them at all."

"Well, I felt sorry for that old man. I do realize that he was going to try and have his way with her, but I thought there might be another way to stop him. She never even tried to talk him out of what he had in mind."

Mom was very upset at Wind and said, "Wind, what in the hell is wrong with you? She's a young woman that some men wanted to force themselves on and who knows what else? As you know, there is no law here in the west and we all have to fend for ourselves, especially women. Don't criticize us unless you have walked in our shoes. I was raped and believe me it is not something I ever want to happen to me again. I'd kill anyone that tried, and so would my lovely daughter. She's right, sleep in the fucking barn."

"I will and I'll leave tomorrow morning. All you women can think about is killing someone. I lived with the tribe all my life and that is all they talked about. When will all this killing stop? Why can't you people talk your issues out instead of killing one another. I for one, am sick of seeing death and destruction."

Mom was now really pissed, she calmly said, "Well, if that's the way you feel, why didn't you let that Indian brave have his way with you? Annie told me all about what you had to go through with that man. He wanted to have sex with you, why didn't you let him? Was it because he didn't belong to your tribe? Did you just try and talk him out of it, how'd that work out? Or was it because you'd have killed him if he tried to rape you? It's no different with a man and a woman, no one likes to do something they're forced into doing. You know, you probably messed up the best thing in your life having told Annie what she should have done. I doubt very much if she'll ever want to spend time with you again. She would have been the best thing you'd ever have had in your life but you're so stupid you messed it up. Now get outta here."

Wind walked to the barn rehashing everything that was said. He was now sorry he told me about the brave that wanted him for sex, it made him appear weak. He told his mother about the episode and she in turn told their chief. The brave was killed shortly afterwards. Not only killed but he was tortured. The tribe would not tolerate such things and the cost of doing it was immediate death. He had felt so sorry for that brave, but he would not have let the man have his way with him. He knew all the tribe looked upon him as weak and almost ladylike. But he himself knew he was not like that; he abhorred the thought of having to do that with a man. *'Oh shit,'* he thought to himself, *'What have I done? Sue was right! It was no different than what had happened to me. I hated that man, and I was glad he was dead; he could no longer come after me.'* Wind went into the barn and prepared to leave in the morning. Before leaving he wanted to talk to me about what he had said.

I was walking a long way from our home, looking and waiting for a deer to come into my sights. I sat for a long while before hearing some whimpering coming from a log nearby. I walked close and saw a wolf carcass of bones and fur laying near the log. As I approached, two baby wolf cubs came scurrying out from behind the log and ran to me. I was stunned to say the least. I had heard that wolf cubs were fearful of humans and every other animal too. They were happy little guys and I sat down and enjoyed scratching and playing with them. They clearly were not afraid of me; in fact, they were treating me like their mommy. I thought it would be best if I just left them be. I got up and began to walk away, but they just followed me. They were so cute, but

I wondered what they have been eating since their mother died. Then it dawned on me, that just maybe they were feasting on their mom. It kind of made me sick just thinking about it but they were animals and they were probably very hungry. Just then a badger appeared by the carcass and began chewing on it. I then realized my new little friends were not cannibals. They tagged along with me all the way home. I did wait for them along the way but not for too long. They do have short little legs.

As I approached my home with my new little friends tagging along, I saw Wind standing by the barn. He walked over to me and said, "I see you have a couple of new boyfriends. A handsome pair I might add."

I smiled at him before saying, "Yeah, they are very handsome, much better looking than my old boyfriend. Where are you going?"

"I'm leaving here for places unknown. Before I left, I wanted to apologize for the things I said. After talking to Sue and rethinking about some things that happened to me personally, I realized how stupid my remarks were. You are a wonderful, beautiful woman and I'll miss you so. I know I can't compete with your new boyfriends, so I'll have to leave. So, this is goodbye."

I was stunned, I fumbled with my Winchester and then looked down at my new boyfriends and smiled. I responded, "I don't want you to leave us now. Just because I found some new boyfriends, I'd still like you to stay. I'm sorry I got so mad, but I hate being looked at as someone that can be taken advantage of. You should know better than anyone, I have not even gotten close to having sex yet. I want to, but I clearly don't want a baby just yet. I have a little sister that still needs me and young Andy. I now also have these two little new boyfriends of mine. I'm afraid, however, you and I are just going to be friends."

Wind walked over to me and said, "Does that mean I'll have to sleep out here with your new boyfriends?"

"No. But all of you boys can sleep on the floor in the cabin. The two little boys can only be in for little while. When they get big, they're on their own, outside."

Wind and I walked up to the cabin with my two new boyfriends following close behind. I named one of the little tykes Boy and the other one Friend.

CHAPTER TWENTY-FOUR

MOM

It was a hard winter and we had so much snow that the little wolves had a hard time getting around outside. Believe it or not, we had them house trained within a couple of weeks. I just couldn't let those little buggers sleep outside in this kind of weather. They were such good dogs, oops, I mean wolves. But they were like all the dogs we ever had. Finding them so young and having our old dog Eagle, helped them to assimilate from a wolf's life to living with humans. They were also very protective of Addie-Lou and Andy and would growl at anything outside our cabin at night. I was a little worried at first and wondered if they'd behave themselves around a small child like Addie-Lou, but they did. When they got to be around six to eight months old, they wanted to be outside all the time. They ventured into the woods every day and when they came back, they never seemed hungry, so we all assumed they were finding some wildlife to eat. When I killed a deer, they would eat whatever we gave them from the kill, but that's about all I had to give them.

In the spring, I started to realize that Mom was not quite herself. She had lost some weight, but she was still as beautiful as ever. The weight loss continued and as summer was on us, she grew weaker. She knew she was sick but couldn't figure out what it was that was slowing her down. I did all the work around the cabin and I got very little help from Wind. I realized then he was one lazy Indian. He would hunt with me occasionally, because he liked to be outside, but he refused to gut an animal after a kill. He said that gutting an animal made him sick. But I told him everyone feels that way when gutting an animal. He still refused, and I was getting pretty sick of him. After listening to his sissy excuses all the time, I began to hunt with Andy and just the two wolves. I'd take Andy along often and he was a better hunter than Wind was, and he would also help me gut our kill. Eagle was getting old, so we left him at home.

One afternoon in late summer, Mom asked me to sit down in the cabin, she had something she wanted to tell me. She began, "Annie, I'm very sick. I'm bleeding from both ends and I'm so weak all the time. I know you've noticed that I can't keep my food down any longer. I'm sure now that I'm dying. What I need to know from you is, that you'll take care of Addie-Lou and Andy? I worry about them so. As I look around our homestead, and I realized the place has gotten very old and is falling apart. You'll need to leave here in the near future. You will never be able to make the repairs needed to live here and Wind would never be of any help. With that being said, there is a lot of gold and silver coins in the hiding place. After I pass on, take all the coins and other valuables and head for a town or some kind of settlement. Please be careful and watch out for Indians and outlaws. Annie, you will have to work with Andy on shooting that small revolver. And just maybe Wind could learn to shoot the Colt or the Winchester. You'll need all the help you can get to protect our family. Now, that's all I wanted to say. Just know I love you so very much."

I was crying like a little baby as I looked into Mom's sad face. I stood up and walked over to her and hugged her. When I hugged her, I realized just how skinny she had become. My poor mom was clearly dying.

It was late October when Mom finally passed on. She had guessed she was around forty years old. The last month of her life was pure torture for her. She was so sick and frail but always had a smile on her face. Wind and I began to dig a place to put her remains and it was a tough job with the ground nearly frozen. Wind complained all the time that the ground was too frozen to dig, so he abruptly stopped digging. What a man? Addie-Lou had not spoken a word since Mom's passing. It had been two weeks and she just sat on Mom's bed and stared into space. She had never cried and never uttered a word. I was worried about my little sister, she was the most outgoing, vocal little kid in the world.

I had enough of the non-talking to last a lifetime and I finally sat next to her and said, "Addie-Lou, your sulking and sitting here looking into the air will not bring Mom back. You have to go on with your life, Mom would want you to. So, cut this shit out right now and get back to being my little sister!"

That's all it took. She began to cry uncontrollably, and she hugged me so hard I thought I'd burst. She said over and over again. "Annie don't leave me, please don't leave me. I need you; I need you. What are we going to do? Will you take care of me?"

That little shit had me crying like a baby, I finally was able to say, "I'll never leave you, you're my sister. You go where I go. Don't you ever worry about that, I promise I'll always take care of you." My goodness, she's so sweet and so beautiful, she reminds me so much of Mom.

Addie-Lou, Andy and I spent most of the winter outside. Watching our wolves run around and wrestle with one another was so much fun. Addie-Lou and Andy were protected by Boy and Friend, and they kept an eye on both of them all the while they were outside. Our other pooch Eagle had died about the same time as Mom had. Our roof was leaking, and we had holes between the logs on the walls and it was really cold inside that cabin. One side of the barn had caved in and we had to move the wagon out of there. We went through all the guns and ammo and we brought the ones we wanted to keep inside the cabin. We were preparing to leave in the spring.

Spring came early on top of our hill and we had decided to leave when all the snow was gone. Before leaving, we all spent some time at Mom's graveside. It brought renewed tears to all of our eyes, but we knew we'd have to leave and move on with our lives. I think I am now around eighteen or nineteen years old and Addie-Lou is six going on eighteen. Andy thinks he's eleven but maybe younger. We don't care how old Wind is.

CHAPTER TWENTY-FIVE

NEW FRIENDS

We didn't have any idea where there was a settlement other than Settlers Gulch, and we knew we'd not be welcomed back there. So, we headed further west. As we rode through Indian territory, we saw many war parties, some we hid from, but others saw us and let us pass. I thought maybe the tribe was letting us pass because we brought the traders back to them. Wind said I was being a bit naive. He knew them all better than I did, and he thought we appeared not to have enough valuables for them to bother with. Little did they know we did. Or maybe it was because of our wolves, Boy and Friend. I told Wind it must be big medicine for us to be traveling with two wolves. He couldn't agree, he said empathically that I didn't have a brain in my head if I thought the tribe cared anything about two little wolves. I quickly responded, "Yeah, I may not have a brain in my head, but you clearly don't have a pair of balls in your pants. You are the biggest coward and laziest asshole I've ever seen. Don't plan on staying with us very much longer, I can't stand you."

We rode for several weeks and my butt was getting sore sitting on that hard seat on our wagon. Wind said he wouldn't drive our team; it wasn't Indian like and it wasn't manly like either. So, Addie-Lou, Andy and I drove the team. Well, I drove the team and my little sister told me continuously what to do. She also told Wind and Andy what to do. That little kid is so much fun.

After putting in over ten hours of riding one day, we stopped for the night and set up our camp. Now, Wind grew up in an Indian camp, so he said he knew the ins and outs of camping. The fire was to be small or none at all. So, if we had a rabbit or a fowl to eat, we'd cook it quickly on a big fire and then distinguish the fire quickly. It all made sense.

However, some other travelers saw our fire. Our wolves were on high alert and warned us of the impending dangers. I grabbed my Winchester and put out the fire. We had Addie-Lou and Andy get under the wagon with the wolves. I hushed at the wolves to be quiet and they stopped their growling immediately. Then we waited. Soon a rider entered our camp, followed by a wagon.

The rider said, "We mean you no harm. Please don't be alarmed, we're just travelers and we need some food. We're starving."

Wind said, "Come on in and stay a while, we do have some food."

After Wind had said that I slugged him in the arm. I whispered, "You stupid bastard, we don't know anything about these people, and we can barely see them in the dark. You keep that Winchester aimed at these people until we know they mean us no harm. Do you understand?"

The rider got off his horse and tipped his hat to me and said, "Thank you so much for trusting us, you are the first people that we have met that have done so. My wife and my two kids are in or wagon."

I looked up to the driver's seat on the wagon and even with just the moonlight, I could see a very handsome boy sitting by his mom. I mean, a man, he was definitely a man. His mom stepped down first, followed by the prettiest young girl I'd seen in a long while. Who in the hell are these people? After the mom got to the ground, she smiled at us and said, "I'm Maggie and this here is my daughter Mary. My husband is Jim, and this is my son is Mark. Our last name is O'Neil. And your names are?"

Wind was very polite and set his Winchester against our wagon and walked towards the lady with his hand extended and said his name was Wind. He shook her hand and then headed towards the stunning Mary. I could tell he was smitten by her right away. He then moved over to Jim and then on to Mark. All the while I stood with my Winchester still in my hands. The wolves didn't know what to do, they just sat by Addie-Lou and Andy and stayed still. Everyone appeared very friendly, but I was still very pessimistic. Wind said "This here is Annie and her sister Addie-Lou and Andy and our dogs Boy and Friend. Well, they're not dogs, but as you can see, they're wolves. Don't be afraid of them they are very friendly once you get to know them. Where are you folks headed?"

Jim said, "We're not sure. Someone a while back, well, a long while back, told us we should try and find a place called Coulson. We heard it's not a town yet, but a man named Coulson has been instrumental in getting a fella named Alderson to build a sawmill there and someone else is starting a general store. This Coulson person and his three brothers own and operate the Coulson Packet Line, which is a steamboat line that is located there. Evidently, they run their boats back and forth on the Yellowstone River, the Missouri River and the Ohio River, to and from some places called St. Louis and Pittsburgh but I can't remember where else. They say the passenger traffic is immense since gold has been found in that area as well as further west. The new community is on the Yellowstone River."

I asked, "How'd you remember all of that?"

He responded, "Since the place is very important to us, we've talked about it every day and we all agreed we should remember all that was told to us."

"Why this place, isn't there many other places you could go to?"

"You are correct, but this one might offer jobs for all my family. It's a start up town and I'm a carpenter as is my son. We felt if there were a store or other places like that, our women could work too. Where are you folks headed?"

Wind quickly said before I could answer, "I think now we'll go along with you folks to Coulson. Sounds like it's a place for us to buy some land and farm or raise some cattle."

I looked at Wind and laughed and shook my head before saying, "Are you nuts? What skills do you possess that would make you think for one second that you could handle that? You are not a farmer, nor a cattle rancher. Besides that, you are the laziest man I've ever seen. You're an Indian, born and raised. Maybe next you'll want to pan for gold?"

I could tell I hit a nerve with Wind. I didn't realize at first how infatuated he was with little Miss Mary. She was good looking but was likely not to be very worldly or able to fend for herself. I fact, I doubted if anyone in this family could fend for themselves. I thought this is what we didn't need, having a family tag along with us that needed us for protection. Wind couldn't handle an attack nor could any of these people, it would be up to me. Shit, they said they were starving. They were like my family coming out west, very ill prepared. But I know I pissed off Wind. I just couldn't help myself, I guess I should have kept my big mouth shut. But screw him, I just don't care.

Wind said, "Thanks Annie, you really know how to make a person feel ill-equipped to face the future. Yes, I grew up an Indian, but I'm not one now. I'm a lot whiter than I am an Indian. I feel I can learn to do anything. Just maybe Mr. O'Neil can teach me carpentry?"

"Wind, I'm so damn sorry for what I said, if you weren't so lazy you could possibly learn a trade. I'm sure of that. I'm thinking this is where Addie-Lou, Andy and I leave you all. I'm not sure I want to go into another situation like we had in Settlers Gulch. That place called Coulson could be just that. Maybe you should get our new friends some jerky and some left over cold potatoes. I'm sorry all of you had to hear our exchange. As you could hear, Wind and I have not gotten along lately and I can't stand his lazy personality any longer. It's time for me and my family to move on."

Maggie said, "I'm sorry if we brought this on. Please forgive us, we'll leave you in the morning."

Wind spoke up, "Nonsense, we talk like this all the time. Annie is not leaving us; these are her idle threats. Sit down and eat so we can get acquainted."

I walked to our wagon and asked Addie-Lou and Andy to come out. They both crawled out as did both of our wolves. They must have felt good leaving the confines and security below our wagon. Mary walked over to see the wolves and said hello to Addie-Lou and Andy. They both seemed to like her, and Andy said, "You're very pretty." The wolves just growled, and I told them to shut up, which they did.

Mary said to me, "Do you dress like that so men will think you're a boy? I thought about doing that, but Mom wouldn't hear of it."

I was stunned. I look like a boy. A boy? I didn't know how to respond to her. Wind walked close to us and said, "Those are her riding and traveling clothes, but they do make her look like a boy or a man. She does have a dress but why wear it when you're on the road?"

He was lucky, and she was also lucky that I didn't shoot her. But I couldn't do that to the pretty Mary. I just turned and walked away.

As I was walking away, I heard Mary say, "I hope I didn't insult her."

My friend Wind replied back to Mary, "No you can't offend her, she is more like a man than a woman. But be careful of what you say in front of her, she has a red-hot temper."

After hearing Wind's comment, I was so hurt. I walked a long way away from our camp. I had my Winchester along with me and I thought if Wind were here, I shoot him. What a friend? I'm more like a man than a woman. That's his view of me? I wonder if he thought I was a man all the times we kissed and fondled each other up? I should ask him about that. I stayed out on the prairie all night by myself. Well, I wasn't quite by myself. Both Boy and Friend found me later that night. They kept me warm.

The next morning Wind found me, and the wolves sleeping soundly and he said, "Wake up, it's time to move on."

I woke up and was trying to get my bearing on where I was. Then it came to me and I remembered what he said about me. He came over to help me up and I said, "Get the hell away from me. I don't ever want to see you or hear from you ever again. I'm more of a man than a woman? Is that what you thought when you were kissing and rubbing me all over. You thought you were with a man?"

I then began to yell so everyone near the wagon could hear, "Why did you have that brave tortured and killed, all he wanted was some sex with you? He must have thought you were a little girl, or did he know you were a boy? Go tell your Mary that story and see if she'll still like you. Wait a minute, would you like me to tell her? Asshole!"

Wind stood motionless and said nothing. I then said, "Addie-Lou, Andy and I are taking the wagon and all the gold and silver with us. Don't follow us and don't say another word to us ever again. I knew this day was coming and here it is. I hope when you and your friends are attacked you grow a pair of balls and try and protect them. Something you were never able to do for me."

I walked back to the wagon and hitched up the horses, got Addie-Lou and Andy aboard and we walked away without saying a word to Wind's new friends.

CHAPTER TWENTY-SIX

COULSON

Wind didn't know it yet, but I took his Winchester along with us and I left him an old long rifle. He did have a Colt, so screw him, the Winchesters were all mine anyway. Addie-Lou, Andy and I didn't know where we were headed but I knew it was west. I was having a great time being with just my little sister and my new little brother and the two wolves. We laughed and laughed at each other and it was kind of like when it was just Mom and me. I miss her so. I now think Addie-Lou and Andy look at me like I'm their mom, which I don't mind.

We came upon a very large valley around four weeks after we left Wind and his new friends. Down at the bottom of the valley ran a very large river and I assumed it was the Yellowstone River. Thus, we must be entering into the Yellowstone Valley. I can't explain the beauty of all the surrounding area, it was magnificent. There was a path for the wagons, and we walked our team slowly down into the valley. When reaching the river, I noticed a small settlement, which I assumed was the future town of Coulson. We rode into the main street and looked around. Close to the river, there was a small hotel and I guessed it was for the travelers from the boats on the river. I saw a general store and a livery stable. We stopped at the store and I had the wolves get into the back of the wagon. I told them to stay, and I hoped they would.

We were getting some looks from the men that congregated around the front of the store. I thought it was because of the wolves but then I realized it was because of me. Me being a woman and all. Addie-Lou, Andy and I got close to the door when a man said, "Mam, I'd like to ask you a question. What do ya charge?" After his comment, all of the men standing there began to laugh.

I stopped in my tracks and told Addie-Lou and Andy to wait inside the store, which they did. I asked the slovenly man, "What exactly are you asking me for?"

He replied, "For a night in the hay with you, that's what I was asking, what do you charge?"

I said, "You know, the last man that asked me that same question, lost his balls, is that what you'd like too? Believe me when I say this, I was happy to oblige him and I'm guessing he didn't live very long after that."

The man walked close to me and reached up and grabbed one of my breasts. He said, "Now, that is more like it."

I quickly pulled my Colt revolver out of my holster and whacked him across the side of his head with the butt-end. He stumbled back and was bleeding profusely from his wound. I quickly holstered my Colt and drew out my Bowie knife from its sheath in my boot. I walked slowly towards the man and placed my knife between his legs and gently lifted it up. I whispered, "I charge two balls and one small wienie. I'll take the balls and wienie with me. Say goodbye to them you asshole."

The man pleaded, "Please don't do that, please don't. I'm sorry, so sorry. I promise I won't do that ever again."

As I was standing there with my knife under his balls, I realized there were two wolves standing next to me growling and all the bystanders had moved away. I finally said, "If I ever see or hear from you again, I will have my two wolves tear you apart. Got it? You stay clear of me." The man turned and ran away. The others did the same.

I told the wolves to return to the wagon, which they did immediately. I then walked into the store.

Addie-Lou and Andy were sitting on a bench near the counter and were talking to a very nice older gentleman. He said, "I'm glad to see a strong woman around here for a change. These men are fools, and they wonder why women hate them. Well, what can I do for you?"

I smiled at his comments, "We need a place to stay, a place to bathe, and a place to eat. I also need a place to store my wagon and stable my horses. Can you help me out?"

"Why yes I can. The hotel has rooms and a place to bathe and eat. I'll get the blacksmith to store your wagon and take care of your horses. Now is there anything in here you'd like?"

I said, "Yes, do you have any ladies' dresses? I need a couple of them. I need some clothes for my little sister and my little brother here. We need new boots, hats, jackets, underwear, two pairs of long-johns, two pairs of dungarees and shells for a Winchester rifle. Also, bullets for a Colt 45. I'll also need a couple of canteens."

"You need a whole lot of things. When you came in, I didn't think you'd need anything. By the way, I'm Vince, follow me."

We found everything we needed; I couldn't believe a store in this wilderness could be so stocked with items. Vince told us, that with all the ship traffic on the river, people needed things and he's here to accommodate them.

After I gave him the silver coins for our purchases, I asked him if there were any properties for sale. He said, "There is plenty of raw land for sale and it's cheap. The only problem is the winters get very cold out here. If it's property with a cabin you want, I have just the place if you have the money."

I replied, "I don't know if we're staying here or not. I have some money and I guess we could look at it, how far away is the property?"

Vince said, "Look, this town has plenty of possibilities. With this store and the boats moving people into the area, it could be a boom town soon. Owning some property is the best thing you can do for your little brother and sister. Once you see the place I'm talking about, I know you'll stay. It's about ten miles out of town up the mountain, overlooking the river. By the way, what are your names?"

"I'm Annie Crow and this is my sister Addie-Lou and my brother Andy. What time tomorrow?"

"How about eight tomorrow morning, right after breakfast. I'll have Roland Muster, our blacksmith, come over and get your wagon and horses. You'll have to send those wolves away until tomorrow."

"I was going to have them go into the wild until tomorrow morning, I just hope some of these idiots don't try and shoot them. See you tomorrow."

Before we left the store, I made sure I had my saddle bags with the gold and silver with me. I sometimes forgot to take them out of the wagon before going to sleep. Addie-Lou, Andy and I then went to the hotel and checked in. The was a room on the third floor with a window facing the street. It had a lock and key, which is something I wanted. We also found the bath area on the first floor and the tub was filled with hot water. It was so refreshing to take a bath in a tub. I had never done that before and neither had Addie-Lou. We did, however, have to bathe together in the same tub. We laughed and really enjoyed ourselves. Andy bathed after us, but they didn't change the water. We all ate dinner in what was called a dining room, again it was the first time for all of us. Someone served our food and refreshed our water cups. We felt we were being pampered for the first time ever. I did wonder what happened to Wind. I was hoping he was doing well with pretty Mary. I hope he didn't screw that up. I always liked him, but I never loved him. Too bad, it was so convenient having him around the cabin, if he hadn't been so lazy. I don't know what I'm doing looking into buying a place. I don't know much about the town and can I take care of a place all by myself? I'll look at the place and see if it will be safe for a young woman and two children to live there. I am clearly in a quandary about this. What will I do?

CHAPTER TWENTY-SEVEN

NEW HOMESTEAD

We met Vince in front of the store at the assigned time, eight o'clock. He had retrieved our wagon and horses from the livery stable and we hopped aboard. Vince rode his horse, and he was quite chatty all the way to the property. He was doing the best job of salesmanship I've ever seen or heard. When we reached the property in about an hour and a half later, I could see what he was so eager to talk about. The place was fantastic. It was not a log cabin like we had with Mom and Crow, but a wooden cabin. It had two glass windows and even a small porch in front. There was a small barn, a corral and a small bunkhouse for the ranch hands to live.

Addie-Lou, Andy and I walked around the entire area and then went inside the cabin. It wasn't really a cabin but a house. I had never seen a place like this before. The inside had a very large fireplace, three bedrooms, a small kitchen with six chairs, a nice table and a wooden floor. A wooden floor! I never, dreamed that anyone would put a wooden floor in a house. We might be the only people in this country with a wooden floor. There was a wood burning cooking stove. All the furniture came with the place. Even the bunkhouse was supplied with furniture. Now came the part I was worried about, the cost.

Vince quietly said, "The folks that built this place left to go back east. Jim and Sandy Anderson were their names and they also had five boys. Jim got sick about six months ago and he and the boys convinced Sandy to move back home to St. Louis for better medical care. The boys hated it out here in the west. I bought the place from the Anderson's. Now I won't tell you what I paid for the place, but let's just say I bought it cheap. Very cheap. There is about fifty acres of land here and with the buildings and furnishing, I can let you have all of it for seven hundred dollars. There will be no dickering, the price is nonnegotiable."

I was stunned, I thought the place would be offered at around a couple a thousand dollars or even more. I was trying to figure out the cost in my head. I said to Vince, "You own the store, what do you think the price of a one-ounce gold coin would be?"

Vince replied, "I know exactly what it is, eighteen dollars and twenty-five cents an ounce. Why do you ask?"

"I'm pretty good at arithmetic, my dad's friend Ted Boran, taught us all about it. Now, the way I figure it, I'll need around forty-one gold coins for this transaction, is that how you have it figured?"

"Shit, I don't know, I'm just a store clerk. It's whatever you say."

"Well, forty-one gold coins at your price would be seven-hundred and thirty dollars. I'll take it. I've got the coins with me now, let me get them out of my wagon and I'll meet you in the house."

Vince was smiling ear to ear, he said, "Young lady, when I first saw you, I didn't think you had a pot to pee in or a window to throw it out of and here you come up with seven-hundred in gold. You better not let anyone else know you got that kind of money."

I smiled and said, "Now I have the pot to pee in and the window to throw it out of. Please keep this transaction to yourself. One last thing, could you get my belongings from the hotel and bring them back here with the deed I need to sign for ownership?"

"Annie, no one will ever know that you have some gold stashed away. And as far as the property goes, I don't want anyone to know that I bought it and sold it. Between you and me, I only paid three hundred for it. They wanted out and they wanted out right away and I was the only person with cash. Now, I'm telling you this because I don't want any of those lowlifes in town to know I have some gold too. This is a rough and tumble area of Montana. It's going to get better in the very near future, but right now there is no law. What you did to that miner yesterday, sent a message to the men around town to leave you alone. You are no run of the mill woman we normally get around here. Most of the women are ladies of the night, you know whores."

I said, "Maybe I should not have bought the property or maybe I should have low balled you." I looked at Vince and his smile had left his face, so I said, "Vince, I'm just kidding. I would have paid a lot more, so I'm happy with the price and with the house. I can take care of myself, as you saw yesterday. I'm not worried about some drunken cowboys. I'm so happy with the way you handled this for me. Please take care and get back soon with my things from the hotel, my deed and my change."

Vince was smiling again, and he said "I'll be here before eight tomorrow morning. I take care of all the property purchases and sales for the Montana Territory here in the Yellowstone Valley. So, I'll have everything you'll want tomorrow."

The next morning, I heard the wolves yapping outside the house and sure enough it was Vince. He was early, almost two hours early. He had everything from the hotel, the deed to my new property and my change. He had to pay the hotel for our night stay and our bath and dinner. That cost us a whopping one dollar and fifty-five cents. He told me he gladly paid the bill as our housewarming gift. Nice man that Vince.

We settled in our new home that first night. We all had our own bedrooms and we let the wolves sleep in the house with us. I wanted their protection in case someone tried to break in.

Andy had a smile on his face from morning to night. He was so happy. It was the first time in his life he had a family that loved him.

He was such a cute little guy, with dark brown hair, blue eyes and big dimples in both cheeks. It had been a long time since he had a family. Things were looking up for all of us, we hoped.

CHAPTER TWENTY-EIGHT

THE O'NEIL FAMILY

We had a surprise visit from Vince a month or so after we moved into our new home. He got off his horse and rapped on the front door. It was about six o'clock in the morning and he had a worried look on his face. He came to warn us that a wagon with several people came into town yesterday afternoon. They had come into the store to buy food, a very small amount of food since they had little money. They asked if a young woman and two little children came through our town. They had described all of us to perfection. He told them he hadn't seen anybody that looked like that. It had to be Wind and his new friends. I asked, "Where are they staying?"

Vince said, "Just outside town in their wagon. I told them that was a poor place to stay, too many thugs around that prey on inexperienced people. They did not heed my advice, however. They appeared to be very poor and down on their luck type of people. The women were very pretty, too pretty for Coulson. Every man in town came in asking about them. They should get the hell out of our town immediately before their accosted, like you were."

"When you go back, tell them where I am, and if they want, show them the direction to take to get here. I know them and I'm sure they'll need my help. Thanks Vince, I'll see you soon, I'm sure I'll need more blankets, food and ammo."

About five o'clock that afternoon the wolves were in a tizzy, they came scratching and growling at the door. I grabbed my Winchester and walked out. There was Wind and his new family, all looking haggard and hungry. I said, "Hello, you are all looking well. Did you have a great trip?"

Wind was mad and he was trying to stay calm, he said, "You took my Winchester and all the silver and gold coins. You left me with nothing."

"I left you with what you came to our home with, nothing. The gold and silver are mine and Addie-Lou's, you had nothing to do with it. You didn't even know our Dad, so how could you claim our gold and silver? And the Winchester, I don't remember you ever having anything to do with that weapon. Crow stole it and everything Crow stole is now mine and Addie-Lou's, not yours. Now, what do you folks want?"

Wind was very angry now, "What do you mean, what do you folks want? We want a place to stay and some food. I can see you have all that we need. Come on Annie, don't be a bitch!"

"Your friends are welcome to stay for a few days, you, however, are not welcome."

Jim O'Neil said, "We'd appreciate it if we could all stay, including Wind. We won't be any trouble, and it appears you have lots of room. Please Annie, let us stay."

"Like I said, you and your family can stay for a few days, but he is not welcome now or ever. I'm through protecting that fool. If you don't like what I just offered, all of you can just leave. This is not a house of charity or a church."

The O'Neil family looked perplexed, and they were lost for words. The offer I made to them was a difficult one to ascertain. If they told Wind to leave, they'd look like they were abandoning him. If they left with him where would they all go? They had no money and no place to stay and the women would be open game for the outlaw men in the area.

Mary was the one that finally spoke, she said, "Annie, I know you're upset about the clothing thing I said, and the comment Wind said about you being more man than woman. He and I are so sorry we said what we said. We didn't think before saying those things. Wind and I have become very fond of one another since we met. We can't be apart, we're in love. Please let us all stay, we'll work for our keep and we'll stay out of your way."

I was even more pissed than before. The gall that woman has. I'm supposed to feel bad for her since she's in love. Tough shit. I said, "Well, it looks like you and your Indian lover will be living in the woods, since you can't be apart. He thinks I act like a man, wait until you see him in action, you'll realize he acts like a little girl. The woods, as you can both see, is that away. Lucky for you, you'll have your love to keep you warm."

Mary was stunned, she said, "You're kicking us out? Just because Wind loves me and not you. Get over it! He's my man, not yours."

I replied, "Yes, he's yours, all yours. And Mary, good luck to you." I turned and grabbed Addie-Lou and Andy by their hands, and we walked into the house and I bolted the door. I could hear them all mumbling outside. I knew I had shaken them up and I was wondering if they'd come running back to me.

After about a half hour or more later there was a knock on the door. Maggie was standing there with her hands folded in front of her. She quietly said, "Would you mind if Jim, Mark and I were to stay in your bunk house? We do have about seven dollars in silver coins left we can give you."

I had cooled down a bit and I asked her to come in. Once in, she looked around and said, "I've never been in something as nice as this. Wooden floors, my, I didn't even know they made wooden floors. You must be so happy here!"

I replied, "I don't really know yet, we been here for only a few weeks. You can stay inside. You and Jim can sleep in the last bedroom.

Tell Wind and his girlfriend they can sleep in the bunkhouse with Mark. You don't have to pay me anything, I have some work that Jim and Mark can do to earn your keep. I'm not mad at you or any member of your family, including Mary. It's Wind that I'm upset with. He has been a leech ever since I met him. He has done nothing to pay for his keep and I assume you'll be taking care of him now and the rest of his life."

"Annie, thank you for your kindness. I understand what you're saying about Wind, he is very lazy. But for some reason Mary is smitten with him. I would ask one more thing. Could Mary sleep in the house away from Wind. I'm afraid they might give into temptation and have sex in that bunkhouse. We had an issue with her before, that is why we moved out here. And the first man she meets, she tells us she's in love."

"If she'll sleep on the floor it's fine with me. Just make sure you tell Wind to stay clear of my house and me."

Maggie walked over and hugged me and said, "We'll work hard to help out around here. Jim and Mark can do all the construction work you'll need. Annie, thank you so much, you won't regret it."

I thought to myself as Maggie walked out the door, *'I hope I don't regret this. I do know I'll get the improvements done around here now and it won't cost me much. That asshole Wind, had better stay away from me, however.'*

That night, Maggie and Jim slept in their assigned bedroom and Mary was nowhere to be found. She and Wind must have slept together. Maybe not together but close to one another. Mark must have gotten an ear full listening to Wind moaning in pleasure.

The next morning, I got Addie-Lou dressed and woke Andy. He said he slept good even if it was on the floor. We all walked into the kitchen area where Maggie was making coffee. I said, "Where is your daughter? I guess she is so much in love she couldn't sleep on my floor. I'm telling you Maggie; I am not going to allow Wind to stay here very much longer. You watch, when Jim and Mark begin to work today, Wind will have disappeared."

Maggie replied, "What can we do? Mary is our daughter, and she tells us she's in love, so what in the hell can we do?"

I smiled and said, "Nothing, there is nothing you can do. But there is something you should all understand; this is a tough place to live. The men around here want a woman for only one thing, and I think you know what that is, sex. They will take her and have their way with her. Then they will distribute her around to all their friends and then they will sell her off by the hour for everyone else. There is no law around here and there won't be any in the near future. I was accosted the first day I got here. But I'm experienced and I can handle a gun and a knife. Your future son-in-law cannot. I've bailed him out of trouble ever since I met him. If Mary and Wind leave here to live in town, she will end up being a whore and he will be long gone. When I said he acts like a little girl, he got mad at me. But I think when Addie-Lou gets older she'll be tougher and stronger than him. At least I'm working with her to be like that."

Maggie just shook her head and said, "Oh my, what have we gotten into? The trip out here was hell and Mary was the main cause of it. She cried and cried, because we took her away from a very big disgrace back home. She thought she was in love with the minister of our church. They were having sexual relations, and he was a married man and the father of five children. Our community didn't ask us to leave, they forced us to leave at gunpoint. They didn't, however, ask him to leave, just us. Think about this, he is a fifty-year-old man, that has a daughter ten years older than our Mary. Mary was seventeen at the time. As you can see Mary is a beauty, but she has low-self-esteem and low-self-confidence."

I was stunned. I replied, "Holy shit, what a story. I don't know what to say. Let's all of us talk today about the future of your family.

You can all stay on indefinitely, but we need to set some parameters and if they're broken the consequences will be severe."

Maggie asked if they could all congregate in the bunkhouse and go over the parameters that we were going to set. I agreed and everyone except the little kids should be there, they were asked to remain in the house. I expected some bad language to be used and I didn't want the kids to hear it. I was getting motherly as I grew older.

After everyone was in the bunkhouse, I began, "This meeting really is about you Wind. I don't care if you bone little Mary here or not, but you won't do it in my home. Mary, if you want to stay here, there are a few rules that you must follow. You'll sleep in the house not in the bunkhouse. I'm planning on having Andy sleep in the bunkhouse with Mark and the wolves. You and Wind will have to have your fun in the woods and not in my home. I will not allow you two to have sex where Andy is sleeping. And you Wind, you will work around here just like everyone else. When Jim and Mark start the improvements today, you will work alongside of them. When there is gardening to do, you will help. When there is wood to split, you'll split it. Winter will be upon us soon and everyone including you will help prepare for it, do you understand?"

Wind was getting more irritated by the seconds, he lashed out, "You're just jealous that I found another woman, and a beautiful woman at that. You can't force me to work around here and you can't force Mary to sleep on the floor in the house. So, screw you, you bitch!"

I walked slowly towards Wind and I could see he was getting a bit worried. I quickly drew my Colt so fast out of my holster no one even saw it coming. I put the barrel to Wind's forehead and whispered, "I don't give a shit what you call me, nor what you think of me, but you will leave here right now. If you don't, I will put a slug into that pee brain of yours here and now. You've seen me in action before and you know I will not tolerate bad behavior in a man. This is some of the worst behavior I've ever seen and the only reason you're not dead now, is you were a friend of mine, but you are no longer one. So get the hell off my land, now!"

Wind was sweating and his eyes were blinking repeatedly. He was shaking but he was able to say, "Mary, let's get the hell out of here right now."

Mary was shaken up by the exchange and I think she was finally realizing that Wind was not the man she thought he was. She replied, "Just where do you suggest we go? I'm not living in any woods and I think Annie is right about you, you're one lazy Indian. No, I think I'll stay here with my family, if Annie and they'll still have me." Wind stormed out the door and I was sure we'd never see him again.

After he left, Maggie, Jim and Mary headed for the house. Mark asked me, "Did you ever love that guy? He is a fool, letting someone like you get away."

As I turned towards the house, I had a big smile on my face, Mark likes me. He likes me!

CHAPTER TWENTY-NINE

DISASTER STRIKES

I knew I needed to go into Coulson, and I was worried about doing so. First off, I was worried that my old friend Wind would be around and would be telling men that we were up the mountain and we were easy game. I was also fearful of being accosted by all the of the lowlifes in the so-called town. Vince would do what he could to help us get in and out in a hurry, but it would take some time. One very good thing was, that Mark agreed to come along with me and his dad Jim as well.

We needed to go to the sawmill and get heavy boards for wooden bars for the windows and doors, ones like we had at the cabin in my first home. I also wanted an escape tunnel in the floor of my bedroom where we could crawl out of the house in case of an attack.

I hated leaving Addie-Lou, Andy, Mary and Maggie home alone without any support. Neither of the ladies knew how to fire a rifle and if they were forced to shoot someone, I didn't think they could. Not everyone is capable of doing that. I asked that they all remain close to the house and don't wander around. That request fell on deaf ears.

As we were driving the team and the pack horses down the mountain, I got an eerie feeling that someone was watching us. I looked around several times and saw no one. I wished the wolves were with us. I wanted to take them with, but I thought they'd be better off protecting the family we left behind.

Once we arrived in Coulson, we were met with the same problems, men gawking at me. This time, however, they stayed clear of me. I was in and out of the store within hour while the guys went to the sawmill. We met back in front of the store within three hours of our arrival. The wooden beams and the support studs for the tunnel had been loaded in the wagon. I had already loaded the panniers with blankets, clothing, food and ammo. We were ready for the slow trek up the mountain to our home.

We got home before dark and I'm glad we did. In the yard lay our wolf Boy. He was clearly dead. I jumped off the wagon and ran to Boy. I yelled for Maggie and Addie-Lou. No response. I walked into the house and there on the floor lying in a pool of blood was little Andy. I sat on the floor and looked him over. He had been shot in the chest and had a stab wound in the area of his heart. I heard a loud cry and scream coming from the wooded area behind the house. I ran out of the house and found Addie-Lou sitting behind some trees with our other wolf Friend. Addie-Lou was shaking so hard she couldn't talk. I picked her up and carried her to the yard. By the time we got to the yard Mark and Jim were there and Jim said, "We couldn't find either Maggie or Mary. Someone must have taken them."

I quietly said to Addie-Lou, "Listen to me sweetie, I need to know what happened here. Slowly think about it and tell me."

Poor Addie-Lou was really upset but she dried her eyes on her sleeve and said, "Annie, it was so horrible. They wanted to take me, and Andy got in their way and stopped them. He gave me enough time to run around them and get into the woods with Friend. I hid there while they were looking for me. They saw Friend and chased him as he ran away from me. He and Andy saved my life. After they left, I went into the house and saw what they had done to Andy. And in the yard, is where I saw Boy. He was dead too. I ran back into the woods with Friend and waited for you."

I hugged her tightly and said, "Did you know who they were, was Wind one of them?"

"Wind was with them. There were three others that I've never seen before. Wind was yelling at Mary, saying she was coming with him. The other men wanted me and Maggie. I don't know why they didn't want Andy, but they just wanted me and Maggie. Andy was so brave. When they tried to grab me, he stabbed one of them in his leg with a kitchen knife that he took off the table. I ran around the two men that wanted me and they shot Andy. They almost caught me, but they were really slow older men. They had a wagon and two horses. Wind was riding one of the horses and Mary and Maggie were in the back of the wagon with one of the men. That man in the back was screaming at them telling them the horrible things they were going to do with them tonight. Annie, I'm so sorry I didn't run towards town to find you, but I was so scared."

"Oh Addie-Lou, you did exactly what I wanted you to do, save yourself. Andy was a brave little boy that loved you so much. He gave up his life so you could get away. Now Addie-Lou, I'm leaving to find Mary and Maggie, will you be brave and stay here with Mark and Jim. I have to go right away so they don't get too far away."

Addie-Lou grabbed me and said, "Please come back and bring Mary and Maggie back with you."

"I will sweetie, I will."

Mark said, "I'm going with you. Dad will stay here with Addie-Lou. I'm a good shot and you have another Winchester, don't you?"

"Are you sure you want to come along?"

"Nothing can stop me. Annie, I fought in the war, I know all about fighting and I'm a very good shot. I can't wait to find these losers. Don't forget, they have my mom and my sister."

We mounted our horses and had plenty of ammo for our Colts and our Winchesters. The tracks were very pronounced in the dirt and we both couldn't understand why they were headed this way. It appeared that they were just circling around through the forest and were heading back to Coulson or somewhere close to there. I suggested to Mark that we'd better hurry, I don't think Wind realized that these men were either going to sell Mary and Maggie or just use them for a day or so and finally kill them. Wind is so stupid, I'm sure he thought they would just come along and help him. Addie-Lou said the man in the back of the wagon was shouting what they planned to do with the girls. I'm sure he didn't expect that. I also don't think he would have agreed to take Addie-Lou and kill Andy. I just don't know for sure, love is in fact blind, and I think maybe Wind was in love with Mary and it was his first time.

I had never spent any time with Mark before today and he was one strong hombre. He lifted those beams around like they were twigs. As we were riding, he said he was a sharpshooter in the Union Army. He joined towards the end of the Civil War, but he did see action in many areas of the south. He said, "If we get clear shots, let me handle it. I'm an expert. The first one I shoot will be the bag of shit, Wind."

I replied, "Mark, you don't know me and what I'm capable of. I want you to just back me up. I don't think you understand what I have planned for these men. They are going to die in agony and when I say agony, I mean they are going to be tortured, just like they did to little Andy. I just hope we find them before they go after your mom and your sister."

We saw them in the distance, while it was just getting dark. They started a very big fire, something that Wind would not have approved of. I was wondering now if maybe they had killed him. We tethered our horses and walked slowly through the woods and the brush. We could hear them talking. Two of the men were arguing who would get Maggie first. The other man was arguing with Wind on who would get Mary first. Wind was trying to tell the man that Mary was going to be his wife. The man pulled out a six-shooter and pointed at Wind's face. Wind put his hands in the air and said, "Okay, okay, you win, I get seconds."

I put the Winchester to my shoulder and aimed it at Wind's competition and fired. The shot hit the man in his groin area, exactly where I was aiming. Mark yelled, "If anyone moves, you'll be dead in seconds."

The man I shot was rolling around on the ground in extreme pain, which was good. That would eliminate him from the confrontation. I yelled, "Throw your guns on the ground and then get your sorry asses on the ground away from your weapons. You have exactly three seconds to do so."

It took a little more than the three seconds, but it was close. Mark picked the guns off the ground and put them into the wagon. Maggie ran up to Mark and was crying so hard she couldn't talk. Mary walked by Wind and kicked him in the side as he was lying on the ground. She said to Mark and me, "Thank God you found us. They were going to rape us and then either kill us or sell us. And this pig is the worst one of all." She was pointing at Wind.

I walked over to where the man I shot was rolling around in the dirt and said, "You poor bastard, did that hurt? Roll over so I can have your gun and do it now!"

The man was on his back when I reached for his gun and he grabbed me by my arm and I quickly shot him in the groin area again. He was out like a candle. I took his gun and gave it to Mark. I then said, "Now, all of you boys, on your feet! Start taking off all your clothes, including you Wind. Mark when these boys get all their clothes off, I want you to help me tie them up to those trees. After they've been tied up, get Mary and your mom in the wagon and head for home, I'll be along shortly thereafter."

The men were tied spread eagle to several trees close where we were standing, and they were all completely nude. When all the men, including the wounded one were tied up, Mark left with his family members. It was then I pulled out my Bowie knife. I calmly said, "Which one of you boys killed my little brother? I promise you, that if someone doesn't tell me right away who did it, you'll suffer so much more."

I looked at Wind and I thought for sure he'd rat his buddies out, but he didn't say a word. So, I started with him. I walked up to him with my Bowie knife out and said, "I hope you'll enjoy this as much as I will." I then castrated him without blinking an eye. He screamed like a little baby, which he was. He passed out immediately. I then walked to the next ones. They were wiggling, swaying and trying to get the ropes off their hands and legs. I repeated my question, "Who killed my little brother?"

No one answered, so the next man in line also lost his testicles. As the testicles dropped to the ground Wind came to and screamed, "You're crazy, you're crazy! What is wrong with you, no one killed Andy, we found him that way? And that Mary, she asked me to take her away from you. You're crazy!"

"So, Wind, my little girl friend, have you forgotten about little Addie-Lou? She is well and alive and told me everything. So, on your deathbed, you still can't tell the truth? It's not a problem, I know the truth."

I then turned to the next rapist and said, "Do you want to tell me who killed my brother? I promise I won't take your man parts if you tell the truth."

He shook his head no and as he did, I sliced off his testicles. Now I had four balls-less men hanging in front of me. I started the next phase of my torture with the guy I shot. He was almost dead, he was bleeding profusely from his wounds, so I left him for the creatures of the night. This is grizzly county and those big bears like a fat dinner once in a while before hibernation.

I looked all the rapists over and said, "You boys do know you have another man part left. Who's first?"

One of the men said, "It was Freddie next to me. The kid was protecting his little sister and he stabbed Freddie with a knife. Just look at his leg."

Freddie screamed, "You bastard, I'll kill ya, I'll kill ya!"

I said, "No, you won't." I then shot the man in the head that finally told the truth. I said, "See what happens when you tell the truth you avoid more pain."

The two men that were alive and that included Wind, were bleeding to death. The blood was emptying from their bodies as they were standing there. Wind said, "Put me out of my misery, please."

I said, "No can do. You were responsible for killing my little brother. I can tell you what I'm going to do, however. I'm going to let you live. I hope someone comes along and helps you, I'm fine with that. I do think the chances of that happening is very slim. I think you boys will be dinner for some hungry bears. Good luck to both of you."

I walked over to my horse and rode away. Andy will rest in peace knowing his killers are dead.

I rode for about fifteen minutes in the dark. I finally stopped and got off my horse. I began to cry and I couldn't stop. I sat against a fallen tree and continued to cry. I just couldn't stop. Flashes of Andy's body lying on the floor with his blood everywhere made me sick to my stomach and I puked my brains out. I then thought of Wind and how I used to feel about him. Why had he changed so much? And killing all of those men. Am I sick? What possesses me to act like I do? Is it because I had to be without a family for so long? I cried harder. I thought about what could have happened to Maggie and Mary. I got some relief from that thought; we did save them from all of that. I will never forget what I did to Wind and the other men. I could have just shot them all and walked away. But no, I wanted to make them suffer. Am I a very sick woman? Am I crazy like Wind said? I do know one thing, however, I'll never let anyone try and violate me or Addie-Lou again.

I fell asleep sitting against that log. I had cried myself to sleep. It must have been several hours later when Mark woke me and was saying, "Annie, wake up, wake up, are you alright?"

I was startled as I woke up. I was dreaming that Wind and his friends had me cornered by the trees and they were all yelling who would be first. I was so scared. Mark was looking at me and said, "You are so pretty. Oops, I'm so sorry, I didn't mean to embarrass you like that. You look so surprised."

I said as I yawned, "I am surprised, I didn't think you ever looked at me before. And after what I did tonight, I doubted you'd ever want to look my way again."

Mark laughed and then responded, "I've been looking at you all the time. I'm just kind of a quiet guy. And as far as what you did tonight, I just don't care. I saw you gave it to those boys pretty good. They deserved what you gave them. We are now certain they won't hurt anyone else again. Annie, I told you I was in the war. I saw things I couldn't tell anyone about. I was forced to do things I still dream about, just like you were doing here. You don't know this, but I sat here watching you for a very long time. You cried in your sleep and even screamed. That's when I woke you. I really like you and what ever happened in your past is irrelevant to me. Now let's go home."

Wow, he said he really liked me. I quietly said, "I really like you too. Yeah, we should get moving."

"And Annie, I finished off both Wind and the last man. I shot them in their heads. I thought the gunshots would have woke you, but they didn't. I just thought they'd had enough pain."

I said, "Thanks."

CHAPTER THIRTY

SETTLING IN & MARRIED LIFE

When we arrived back at the homestead it was early morning, but everyone was awake and waiting for us. Addie-Lou was the first one out of the house and as soon as I was on the ground, she hugged me like I never been hugged before. She cried and cried. I did too. After all the tears were shed, she looked at me and said, "Don't you ever go off and leave me again. You stay here where I can see you all the time."

I wiped away her tears with my sleeve and said, I won't leave you again. Now, you and I are going to start to look like ladies again. Let's get our new dresses out and put them on. We'll first go down to the river and take a bath. Whaddya say?"

"I say, let's do it. Let's see if Mary and Maggie want to come along."

Everyone including the men said in unison, "I'm going too."

We all trudged down to the river, which really wasn't a river, but a creek that ran down to the river. It was deep enough for us all to swim and make a lot of noise. I washed Addie-Lou's hair and she washed mine. I looked over at Mark without his shirt on and I smiled. Wow, he is built. I'm not very experienced with men as I've stated before, but wow, he looks so good! Wind was not a very good example of a strong man. He was quite flabby, yes, quite flabby. Mark is not! He's chiseled and when I say chiseled, he is in every way. The hard work he's endured over the years has made a very strong man out of him. Beside he's a real looker, if you get my meaning. I splashed water on him, and he came over softly tipped me over into the water. Boy, did that feel good. I think something in my body has awaken and I don't know if I can rein it in. I've never felt like this before, even with Wind when we were fooling around. I better slow down, the last thing we need is another little kid around here. But I do like kids.

The next three years were not without some difficulties, but overall, everything went quite well. Two years after Wind and his friends tried to take some of our family members from us, Mark and I were married in a family service. Since there was no minister or priest available, Jim married us, and we made up our own vows. Mark and I had been struggling to remain celibate for well over a year and we thought it would be best we marry soon. Everyone moved out of the main house and into the bunk house so we could consummate our marriage and have a honeymoon by ourselves. After two days Addie-Lou was knocking on the door. We let her in and in she remained in.

I was always her mom and now Mark was her dad. She was getting so big and was so smart. I spent every day working with her on her reading, writing and arithmetic. One other aspect of her education that I worked with her every day, was her shooting that small pistol. She was very accurate and loved shooting. She was getting better than her grandfather Jim but was not to Mark's level or mine yet.

We went into Coulson every two weeks for supplies. It was always Mark and me. Mary never ventured into town and neither did Maggie. But they both had enough of men to last them a lifetime. Unless a real nice one came up the mountain, then, maybe just then, Mary might be interested.

We all had our own jobs to do around our homestead. But both Mark and Jim did carpentry jobs occasionally that Vince at the general store would line up for them. The jobs were always day jobs and they would always return home daily. We had a rule everyone was to be home for dinner by six o'clock at night. No exceptions to that rule.

As the years flew by, things got so wonderful. I had my first baby in 1878 when I was twenty-three years old. At least I think I'm twenty-three. Her name is Kathleen or just Kate. I named her after my mother. Mary, Maggie and Addie-Lou assisted in the delivery. Addie-Lou is now eleven years old going on thirty. She is so mature for her age and she never flinched during the delivery. She stayed calmer than Maggie and Mary did. Little Kate is a bundle of joy, however Addie-Lou thought she makes way too much noise. I had to tell her, so did she when she was a baby. I told her I couldn't stand her during that time. She only laughed when I said that. She replied that she was the best baby ever. I did agree that I loved her so, as did Mom. She always asks about Mom. She remembers her, but not like I do. So, I tell her stories about Mom, how beautiful she was, how kind she was and what a good mother she was. I also told her about how I acted when I first met her. Which, I must say, I wasn't very nice. The one person she never asks about is Crow. She already knows he was an outlaw and stole from people and killed many more for their gold and their weapons. She never remembers how much he loved her. And how much he loved me and Mom.

I try and explain to her why I thought Crow was so mean to others, but Addie-Lou has no interest in hearing about those things. What she does like to hear about is my short stay with the Cheyenne Indian tribe. I tell her about the one person that took care of me when I was just a child, Manda. She is mesmerized by my story about the Nose and how I stood up to her. Since I was about her age at the time, she wonders if she could have done the same. I always tell her she would have. But I'm not sure she could have. She's a strong-willed little girl but she is also very loving. I was not very loving at the time. I was living with the sorrow of losing my mom and my three brothers.

Being married to Mark is so wonderful. We do have disagreements, which we always find out later is Mark's fault, not mine. He is so loving and kind. He's also a good father but he will never discipline Addie-Lou when she has done something wrong, whereas I do it all the time. Even grandma Maggie will discipline that little shit Addie-Lou. We have to accept what Addie-Lou says about herself, she perfect.

CHAPTER THIRTY-ONE

MANDA

It is now 1881 and I am now twenty-six years old. Mark and I have been trying like crazy to have another baby, but for some reason nothing has happened. Mark thinks maybe we're trying too hard. He says maybe having sex every day is a strain on him physically and that prevents his sperm from reaching my eggs. I have to remind him that nothing has changed since we were trying to have Katie. We were having as much sex then as we do now. And I for one like having sex almost every day.

Addie-Lou remains as inquisitive as ever. She is now fourteen going on forty and has become a woman. She doesn't like the issues of being a woman, but she now accepts it.

The population in the town of Coulson has grown exponentially, as more and more gunslingers, drifters, miners, gamblers and whores use the steamship line to travel here. The steamships offer much more comfort and security than a covered wagon or horse back. But, as the town has become more lawless, the safety the travelers experienced on the steamships disappears as soon as they step on dry land. Gun fights are a daily occurrence and senseless murders are frequent. If a woman is not escorted by a man, a man toting a gun, she's fair game for any of these gunslingers. So, when we go to town, we have to be very careful. Addie-Lou is not allowed to go to town ever.

Mark and I did our biweekly trip to Coulson to get our needed supplies. We need fruit, which the only fruit we now have on the homestead is apples. We can get jars of peaches and berries that have been preserved in glass jars. Also, vegetables. We always need ammo and we also look to see if any new guns have come to market.

We enter the town normally in the very early morning, when most of the gunslingers and lowlifes are sleeping off a hangover. Vince opens his doors at six AM, and we are there for the opening. After we were allowed in Vince said, "Annie, do you remember an Indian woman by the name of Manda?"

I was stunned, I said, "Why yes, I do. How do you know her?"

Vince looked around the store to see if anyone else was listening before saying, "Well, we had a pretty big thing happen around here yesterday. A couple of lowlife gunslingers, well that's what I call them. They are likely just miners, but they had a woman called Manda in the back of their wagon. There was a young Indian boy in the wagon too. I'm guessing he was about fifteen or so, but young. There were also two other young girls in there too. Well, Manda slid out of that wagon and ran in here with her hands tied in front of her. She had been beaten up pretty good but was still a pretty good-looking lady. She got down on her knees and begged me to help her. She asked if there were any white family's that might help her, she claimed to be white. I told her that there were two white family's up the mountain by the name of Crow and O'Neil. And her eyes went wide open when I said Crow. She whispered, 'Is one of them Annie Crow? If so, please tell her Manda needs her help. Please!'"

Vince looked around again to see if anyone in the store could hear him and he began again, "Her owners, as they claimed they were, came in and grabbed her off the floor. They then slugged her several times in the face and put a rope around her neck and dragged her out of here by her neck. Annie, that poor woman has been abused so bad. She's so skinny, I could tell they're not feeding her and they're selling her off to the other outlaws and miners for sex. Those bastards capture Indian women all the time now and abuse them. Is she really a white woman? If we had some law around here this wouldn't be happening. I don't know what you can do, but maybe you could offer to buy her from those fools."

I looked at Mark and said, "Mark, I wouldn't be alive today without the help I got from Manda. She was with the Cheyenne tribe that killed my family. She was in the same predicament I was in; she was taken as a young girl."

Mark replied, "Annie, trying to take her with us could be very dangerous. In fact, we could both get killed."

"I know. I want you to leave and go home and I'll try and save her."

"No, you won't! You are my wife and I go where you go. Remember, I was a sniper in the war, so you talk to them but before you start shooting make sure you know where I am. I'll only need a small space to kill a man. Let's us go and try and find this Manda."

My goodness, I love my man so much. As we walked down the street, Mark looked me over and said, "You look like a beautiful gunslinger. That blue shirt and tight dungarees and that Colt hanging from your hips makes something inside me stir. And those brown eyes and your hair in those braids. You are all woman." I hugged him and patted him on his round butt.

Since it was early morning, none of the gunslingers or drunks were around. We guessed they were all sleeping off a drunk. Vince told us that the man that had Manda is called Spike. He has two brothers with him, one is nicknamed Roger the Dodger and the other is Foxy. Their last name is supposed to be Young. Spike is the killer of the group, according to the rumors. But his brothers think they're killers, but according to eye witnesses, they are both cowards. They stay close to Spike because everyone in the mining camps is afraid of him. Vince said they hole up close to the river, downstream about a half mile from

Coulson. The word is that Spike can't see very well, actually Vince says he can't see anything unless it's big and right in front of him. The other Young boys can see but have no balls to fight with anyone.

Mark and I walked toward where the Young brothers were camping. After getting close to what we thought was their camp, Mark headed up the hill overlooking their camp. He stood close to a tree and balanced his Winchester on a small branch. I walked into the camp by myself and saw Manda sleeping in a wagon. There was a young man in the wagon with her but no one else. I slowly walked towards the wagon where Manda was sleeping, when I was surprised by the flap of the tent nearby opened and a dirty man stepped out dragging a young woman by her arm behind him. He looked at me and said, "Who in the hell are you and what do you want? This here is private property and you gots no right to be here. You get the hell outta here right now."

Just then another man came out dragging another young woman and he said, "Oh no! You ain't going nowhere. You come right over here, wee's been on the lookout for a good-looking woman like you. You can bring in us some much-needed cash. I said, come over here darlyn and I mean right now."

Just then another person came out of that tent holding a six-shooter in his hand. He said, "Where is she? Bring her close so I can see her."

The man called Roger walked close to me and grabbed my arm. I jerked his hand away and said, "Keep your damn hands off of me. I want Manda! She's the one in your wagon. She's my friend and you are done with her now. If you don't turn her over to me, you'll all die a slow agonizing death. I'm willing to pay you for her and she will be coming with me today."

Roger suddenly grabbed me by my throat and began to squeeze. I quickly drew my six-shooter from my holster fired, the sound was deafening, and Roger's hand came slowly loose from my throat as he dropped to the ground. My shot had hit him somewhere in the chest and I think I may have hit his heart. I'll never know, it happened so quickly. Old Roger wasn't a very good dodger after all. Spike was trying to get his six-shooter out of his holster as I pointed my Colt at him and yelled, "If that six-shooter comes out of that holster, you'll be dead before you can cock the hammer. Go ahead, make my day." I had heard that quote somewhere, but I can't remember where.

Spike said, "You can't come into our camp and shoot my brother you bitch. No sir, you can't do such a thing. It's against the law."

I said, "Neither of you boys look very sorry that your brother just died. What is it, good riddance? One less mouth to feed? And on that law-and-order thing you spoke about. Did you boys know it's against the law to take women for your own pleasure? It's called rape. And then to sell them to others for sex, that's prostitution. All of that is against God's law and the law of the land. Now Manda and the young man and the young girls are coming with me. Understand? Do you two fools understand?"

Spike said, "You can't do that. We own them fair and square. I want one hundred in gold for each one of them. That's five hundred."

I laughed at Spike and said, "Who taught you to count, a man with only five toes? Four of them at one hundred a piece, is four hundred, you dumb ass. You know, I'll pay you the four hundred the next time we come to town. But right now, they come with me."

"What about my brother Roger? We need a hundred for him too. He's worth at least that, ain't he?"

I smiled and said, "No he's not, he's worth about the same as you two, nothing. If you stick around Coulson, we'll be back in a couple of weeks and I'll pay you four hundred in gold. If you come looking for me, you'll get nothing and you'll wind up dead like your brother. Now Manda, get your friends and yourself out of that wagon, you're coming with me."

Manda slowly got out of the wagon, but she was very weak. The young man helped her as did the young girls. One of the young girls walked over to where Spike was standing and spit in his face. He raised his hand to slap her but couldn't see her right away, so I slowly aimed my Colt and shot a bullet into the palm of his hand. That shot shocked everyone but me. Big tough Spike was laying on the ground holding his hand and was crying in pain. I looked at his brother Foxy and he had peed his pants. Yes, they were real tough guys. I strolled slowly over to where the Young brothers were and confiscated their antique weapons and threw them into the river. Foxy screamed, "You'll be sorry for what you done did to my brothers. We'll gets ya."

I walked over to him and said, "Well, aren't you a big bad gunslinger? Well, Mr. Big Bad Gunslinger make your move. I'll even give you a gun to use and I'll give you time to draw first. Then I'll shoot you down like a dog. Are you ready?"

"No sir, you ain't tricking me into no gunfight. You got someone up on that hill looking after ya. No, I ain't stupid"

"Yeah, you're stupid. Yeah, not only are you stupid, but you're also a coward. I'm going to tell everyone I see today in this town, what cowards you Young boys are. Cowards, chicken shit cowards. Yeah, you're real tough guys, all you can do is hurt women and children. If you come looking for me and Manda and her friends, it will be the last thing you'll ever do in this lifetime. Maybe you'll get another chance in hell, but that's doubtful. Now, we'll leave you, if you follow me, you'll die, it's your choice."

I walked with my new friends toward the general store, knowing Mark was following me and watching our backs. When I got to the store Vince came out. I asked if he could help us out and give Manda and her friends a lift to our homestead. He whispered, "Meet me out of town and I'll get my wagon out and help you. No one can know what I'm doing for you, understand?"

CHAPTER THIRTY-TWO

SAFE AT LAST

Vince met us on the outskirts of Coulson and all our new friends climbed aboard. I rode close to the wagon and talked to Manda. She had a big smile on her face and said, "I'm so thankful you found us. I thought me and my grandkids would die at the hands of those awful men."

I asked, "How did they find you? Where were the tribe's warriors? Did they kill the entire tribe?"

Manda laughed at me and said, "You haven't changed one bit, always asking questions, one after another. I've missed you so. But, on to what happened. As you may have remembered, the tribe was infested by those blankets, but it was so much worse than what we thought when you returned those men to us. Our whole tribe of three hundred or more people were almost wiped out. Except for a few of us. I've always guessed that we survived because all of us were white or part white, and we were somehow immune to the disease. There were other mixed-race people that also survived, and we all left in different directions. My guess is that there were over fifty of us in all. We originally had ten of us together and we all moved around to many parts of our homeland and were able to exist on deer meat, fowl, fish, wild berries and wild vegetables. When winter came, we forged through the forests trying to keep out of sight of both

Indians and white people. We lost two of our women to kidnappers and four of our party just left us. We survived for many years until those Young brothers found us. My poor granddaughters, they had the worst time of all of us. They tried to sell me and my grandson several times, but they always wanted too much for us. They were bound and determined to keep my granddaughters, however. And Annie, they will go to great measures to get them back. We have to be very careful."

I sat on my horse in shock. I shook my head and said, "Wow, you have gone through so much. I wish I could have known sooner that this had happened to you. Manda, I so sorry for what you all endured. Your lives will be much better from now on. I now wish I'd have killed all three of those poor excuses for men. If I had, we wouldn't have to worry about them any longer. But we'll be vigilant."

We arrived at home and were met by all of our family members. Addie-Lou was the first out of the house and she was determined to get to know who the newcomers were. She said, "Hi, I'm Addie-Lou, what are your names?"

Manda stepped forward and said, "Why hello Addie-Lou, I'm a friend of your mom's. I'm Manda and these are my grandchildren; this is Walking Woman, and her Cheyenne name is Aameohne'e, we call her just Walk. This is my other granddaughter Ae'enahkohn'e, or in English, She Bear, we call her She. And my grandson Aenoheso, or in English Little Hawk, or just Hawk."

Addie-Lou smiled at the girls and said hello, but she was quite enamored with Hawk. She asked him, "Hawk come with me and I'll show you around."

Hawk looked at Manda and quietly said, "Is that alright grandma?"

Manda replied, "Hawk, you are with friends now, you can do as you like. Would you like to go with Addie-Lou?"

He replied, "Yes, very much so."

Addie-Lou and her new friend walked away. The two girls asked if they could follow Addie-Lou and Hawk and Manda told them to go ahead.

All of the family members got together that night, so we could all figure out what was needed to protect our new family members from the Young brothers and their friends. Mark was in charge of explaining what to do and what not to do. He said, "When we all retire for the night, wherever you sleep, you will make sure all the windows and doors are boarded up. There are escape hatches in both the bunkhouse and the main house. So, if the Young brothers try and break in, or set fire to our buildings we can all get out safely. The tunnels are underground and will take you about one hundred yards away from an attack. There will be weapons for all of you to protect yourselves. Now, my guess is these men are so stupid they'll attack in the morning, when it is light out. Most good soldiers would attack at night. They may, but it is doubtful from what you folks have told us about them. When outside, I'd like everyone to always have another family member with them at all times."

After Mark had finished, it was my turn. I began, "I saw firsthand how unintelligent these men were. Spike will only have the use of one hand, but the other Young, Foxy, will be the one I worry about the most. He's a coward, but he is also a very mean, hateful and disturbed. He will do anything possible to take us women, especially me. So please, always carry a weapon on you at all times. We have holsters and six-shooter for everyone, and we'll start shooting lessons today. One thing to always remember, kill them if necessary, because they will kill you if they have the chance. And, if you kill one of them, please have no regrets or remorse. Let's get onto target practice."

We hadn't seen anyone near our homestead in several months and we were finally getting over the fear of an attack. Mark and I went into town every two weeks as we had for a couple of years and the town was still booming. I asked around about Spike and Foxy, but no one had heard or seen them in a very long time. Vince at the general store, said Spike had stopped in and bought bandages for his wounded hand. It looked to Vince that Spike would lose the use of that hand.

Mark and I wandered out to the Young brother's old campsite and found new tenants at the location. We asked about the Young boys and they said they were pretty banged up and just moved on. They said their brother was shot down like a dog, by a gunslinger named Crow. This Crow fella was someone they'd soon find and would kill him, like he had done to their brother. They also said the same gunslinger had shot Spike in the hand and it left the hand useless. Spike said the same gunslinger named Crow stole their women and all of their gold. They have friends and they'd get together and find this Crow fella.

I smiled at the three men and said, "Did these two Young boys ever tell you that the gunslinger named Crow was a lady? I'm the lady that killed Roger the Dodger Young. I also shot that fool Spike in his hand as he tried to slap a woman. They are both cowards and clearly not the gunslingers they made themselves out to be. They have reputation as gunslingers, but they are just rapist and cowards. If you see them, tell them that Annie Crow is looking for them."

The time seemed to fly by as we all got adjusted to having additional people join our family. Originally, I was fearful that She and Walk would suffer the effects of their stay with the Young boys. But they seemed to adjust to being with us very well. In fact, they were the leaders of the teasing and they both loved Addie-Lou and little Kate. They hung around Mary most of the time as they were close to her age. Hawk, however, was smitten by Addie-Lou. He followed her around most days and sometimes it was too much for Addie-Lou.

Addie-Lou now insisted that we just call her Addie, which was very difficult for me. I loved that name Addie-Lou and I reminded her frequently that she was named after our mom's grandmother. Addie however, told me that I was her mother, she hardly remembered Mom. That was so sad for me to hear, Mom was such a big part of my life. However, I really did like the fact that Addie considered me her mother.

A year has passed since Manda and her grandchildren had joined us. We have quit worrying so much about being attacked, but we are still being vigilant. Maybe the Young boys have screwed with the wrong people and are both dead.

How wrong I was, they were not dead. I'll explain later.

CHAPTER THIRTY-THREE

Best of Times, The Worst of Times

It is now 1882 and there was some bad news coming from the town of Coulson. Coulson residents had been expecting that the railroad would soon be coming to their town. They expected that Coulson would be a railroad hub, and it would become the Territories largest city. How wrong they all were.

The president of the Northern Pacific Railway, Frederick H. Billings knew he could make far more money by creating a new town, which would be named after him; Billings, Montana. At first, the town of Billings had only three or four buildings and it appeared that Coulson would survive as the towns were side by side. However, the lawlessness of Coulson, made it easier for folks to move and establish residency in a boom town such as Billings. Because of the expansion of the railroad to Billings, law and order was a necessity. Lawlessness remained in Coulson and because of it, Coulson would soon become almost a ghost town. A few miners and outlaws remained but most moved further west.

I must say I was happy with the decision of the railroad to move to the area now called Billings. Coulson still had the general store and the livery stable. I expected that soon we'd have to go into Billings for our supplies. That would not be a problem, since it was about the same distance for us as Coulson.

I still haven't been able to get pregnant, but we are still trying real hard. We are loving life here on this mountainside with all our family members. Manda is now the grandmother to both Addie and to Kate. They love her so. Addie and Hawk have become inseparable and I do worry about them getting too lovey-dovey. The girls, that being Mary, She and Walk wanted to go with us into Billings to possibly meet some new friends. By new friends, I mean boyfriends. Mark and I have agreed to take them all along when we next travel to Billings. We have however, told the rest of the family they must stay close by, in case we are attacked.

Two weeks later we left for Billings and I didn't quite know how the girls were going to meet some new friends, or should I just say meet a man. Once we entered the town it was quite evident that finding a man in Billings would be no problem. When we stopped our wagon in front of the general store there were several young men that stopped by to say hello to all the girls. Mark and I entered the store and found it well supplied. It took us about an hour to find all we needed. When we walked out the girls had each found someone they liked. I looked them over and thought to myself, *'these are just boys, not men yet. Well, they're men but just barely. However, our girls have really just turned into women. Maybe we should just see where things go.'*

Mary was the first one to ask, "Annie, would you mind if Howard were to follow us home, so he can see where we live. He wants to be able to find me after today."

I smiled and said, "Of course Howard can follow us home. He seems like a very nice young man."

It took us more than two hours to return home. Once we got home, Mary and Howard walked around our homestead talking and laughing. It was so nice seeing Mary happy again. Wind was such a poor excuse for a man and that minister must have been a real loser too. Just maybe Howard would be good for her.

Manda was cooking a stew in the main house when it happened. A shot rang out close to the bunkhouse, but it didn't hit anyone. Most of the family was indoors but Mark and I were outside. Mark looked at me and said, "Run for the main house and don't look back."

I did as Mark told me to do and I was surprised that he wasn't following me. He was standing between the bunkhouse and the main house holding his Winchester in shooting position. He fired four shots and I heard yelling by at least two men. After the shooting, Mark hightailed it to the main house. Once inside he said, "It's those Young brothers and they have a shitload of men with them. All of them are armed. I shot two of them in their chests and I'm sure we won't have to worry about them any longer. As we were talking, Jim had locked and bolted up the windows and bolted the door. We all had weapons with us except Howard. I looked at him and I could see the panic in his eyes. I'm sure this is not what he had in mind when he wanted to spend time with Mary.

Mark finally looked at all of us and said, "This is going to be an all-out war. Those guys outside are here for the women and I think they also think we have a load of gold. We have the escape hatch and I think we'll have to use it if they yell that they're going to burn us out."

I looked around and I didn't see Addie and Hawk. I shouted, "Where in the hell is Addie and Hawk? Were they outside, I thought they were inside? Where in the hell are, they?"

Manda said, "Annie, they've been gone for a long while now. I'm not sure where they went."

I yelled, "Manda, did they have their guns with them? Oh shit! I've got to get out of here and find them. I'll die if something happens to Addie-Lou."

Mark quietly said, "You and I will wait until dark and then we'll go out the tunnel, but not before dark. I'm sure they heard the shots being fired and they both know what to do. We trained both of them so well. And Addie has her small pistol and a Winchester as does Hawk. They'll both be fine."

I was crying so hard I couldn't speak, when Manda hugged me and said, "Annie, we have worked with our entire family for over a year, preparing for something like this. As you well know, those Young brothers are not very bright and I'm guessing that anyone that would follow them is not very bright either. Our kids are, however."

Mary was standing very close to Howard when he said, "Who are those guys? Did Annie call them the Young brothers?"

Mary responded, "Yes, it's the Young brothers, we're sure of it. Annie had a run in with them a while back. They had taken Walk, She, Hawk and Manda as prisoners and were trying to sell them. Annie killed their brother and shot the one named Spike in the hand. We always felt they may come after us, but it has been so long ago, we felt they must have died or something like that."

Howard replied, "I know those losers. They killed my ma. They kidnapped her on our way out here from back east. We found her alive, but just barely alive two weeks later. She told us it was the Young brothers who took her. She said they bragged about doing the same thing all over the west. Dad and I had left her alone while we hunted and when we returned, she was gone. After she died, we tracked them for about a month to Coulson and then they disappeared again. We were told that someone killed Roger and shot Spike, it must have been Annie that did that. We tried in vain to track them, but we couldn't find their tracks. Dad and I have been waiting around Coulson and Billings for them to return. I can't believe my good luck. Mark, would you mind if I went with you and Annie tonight? I have a score to settle with them."

Mark just nodded his head yes.

As it was turning dark, we heard someone yell, "This is Spike Young! We want your women, and we want your gold. You send out the women and the gold, and we won't burn the place down. If you don't send them out immediately, we'll torch the place. It's your move. We gots lots of men here to help us this time, so you'd better hurry."

As big mouth Spike was talking, Howard, Mark and I were crawling out the tunnel with our weapons in hand. Howard had a six-shooter, and we gave him a Winchester. After getting out of the tunnel, Mark whispered, "Let's wait to split up and all of us move together around to where these boys are waiting. I don't know how many there are, but when I shot those two other boys, it appeared that they had quite a few others with them. We'll have our hands full."

We all walked around to the left. Mark was making a wide sweep and Howard and I were following. We slowly crept towards the bunkhouse. When all of a sudden, a man walked directly in front of us. We surprised him to say the least. He attempted to draw his gun from it holster but he was too late. Mark shot him in the forehead with his Winchester. As we were turning to run away, I heard a voice behind me say, "Mom, it's Addie and Hawk. We're over here."

After hearing Addie say she was over here, I heard a gun go off and saw Mark drop to the ground in front of me. I tried to stand up and get my six-shooter out of my holster, but it was too late. I felt a bullet hit my rib cage and the pain was excruciating. Another shot hit me in my shoulder. I vaguely remember Addie kneeling by my side, when another shot was fired and Addie slumped over me, bleeding from her head. Another shot was fired, and I heard someone say, 'a dead Injun is a good Injun.' As I closed my eyes, I could feel my mind slipping away. But before I was completely out, I heard Howard yell, "Uncle Spike, Uncle Foxy, I got all of them that snuck outside. You can use the dynamite now." The explosion was immense, it shook the ground I was laying on. I then heard Howard say, "Uncle Foxy, I guess we're not so stupid after all? They are!" Laughter followed his comments. After hearing those last words, I think I must have passed out.

I woke up in a wagon that was going over a very bumpy road. I was being jostled around but I had no pain. I was in la-la land. I had no worries, and I couldn't remember who I was or who I was with. I just didn't care. I thought I must be dead and maybe I was headed to heaven. Several hours later, I found out I was not in heaven, but I was in Coulson in the back of the general store in other words, hell.

Vince said, "Annie, Doc Jones is here, and he'll have to take the bullets out of your shoulder and your rib cage. You've lost a lot of blood, but you shouldn't feel any pain. We gave you some Laudanum after we found you at your property and Doc is going to give you some more now. It's pretty bitter shit but it will knock you out." I kind of remember most of what Vince said and that shit was bitter, but after the bitterness I felt so good.

Hours later I woke in extreme pain again and Vince gave me a few drops of that bitter shit again. I was back in la-la land again. Nothing made any sense, I was sure I was dead, and this was heaven, or was it hell? Vince and his wife Mildred, or Doc Jones were always by my bedside. They were trying to tell me what happened, but it made no sense.

Finally, Vince had enough and told me in no uncertain terms I couldn't have any more Laudanum until I could comprehend what had happened. The withdrawal from that shit was horrible. I began seeing things that weren't there and I was reliving things from when I was shot. Vince told me it might take a week or so to get my mind straight.

CHAPTER THIRTY-FOUR

RECOVERY

After a week, I was in so much pain I couldn't think straight. Well, even before that week, I couldn't think straight because of the Laudanum. But at least I felt wonderful. Doc, Mildred and Vince surrounded me, and Vince began, "I'm not sure how much you remember but I'll try and put all the pieces together for you. Some of this is what you told me when I found you and some of it was you rambling on. Are you ready to hear what happened?" I nodded yes.

Vince began, "Annie, you are the only one of your family to survive. Everyone else was either shot to death or were blown up by dynamite. You told me Mark was shot in the head by some guy named Howard, and that you all had just met him. Addie and Hawk were shot close by where you and Mark were shot. It appears that they all died quickly. They left you for dead. You said, this Howard fella called Spike and Foxy his uncles. All of your buildings were blown up by dynamite. There was nothing left of the buildings when Doc and I got up there. They wanted revenge and they got it. I'm sure they don't know that you survived, so maybe we can get some soldiers or the lawman in Billings to help find them. It appeared they didn't want the women, they just wanted all of you dead."

I was very stoic when I said, "What happened to my daughter Kate? Was she killed in the blast too?"

Vince replied, "Annie, I'm afraid so. All your family members perished including little Kate. Those bastards were hell bent on killing everyone, including you. We heard rumors that the Young boys recruited about fifteen men to attack your family. They had told them there was a shitload of gold on your property. However, they found none. They were all pissed off especially since three of their friends died up there."

"Vince, what did you do with the bodies?"

"Annie, we buried them all in one grave and put a marker on the site. I hope that is alright with you, we just didn't have time to bury them individually."

"That is fine and thank you for doing that for me. When I'm feeling better, I'd like to go up to the property, there are somethings I want to retrieve."

Vince said, "Annie I can't imagine the sorrow you are experiencing now. You've lost everyone you loved. We want you to stay here with us until you're feeling better. Will you do that?"

"Yes, I'll stay for the time being while I heal. In the meantime, I want some more of that bitter shit to help me get over my pain."

Several weeks had now passed since Vince told me about how my family had died. Losing Addie-Lou, Kate and the love of my life Mark, put me into a deep depression. I just couldn't think straight, and I needed that bitter shit to help me cope. I thought that maybe it was the bitter shit that was making me feel so down but I just couldn't give it up.

Winter was here and the snow was piling up. Billings was the boom town and Coulson was a doom town. I think it was around 1882 or 1883 and I think I'm about twenty-eight years old. And I think it is my birthday, but I'm never sure. So, my gift from my friend Vince was, "Get off that bitter shit or leave our home. You owe me so much money now and I can't afford buying that shit for you any longer."

So, I left. I had to walk because I had no horse, no money, no future and no bitter shit. So, I walked up the mountainside to my old homestead in the cold and snow. I never told Vince that I thought I could locate our gold supply, but now I was forced to look for it. I also had to face the fact that my family all died there, and I was the only one that survived. It took me almost the entire day to reach my homestead. I am out of shape and I'm facing withdrawal from the bitter shit. I am very skinny, because the bitter shit takes away your appetite. I realized that I'm a mess. I thought, *'What am I going to do if I find the gold stash? Am I going back to Coulson and drowned my sorrows in the bitter shit or am I going to go after the Young boys? Shit, I think it will be easier for me to go back to Coulson and get a new supply of the bitter shit.'*

I slept outside in the cold near the burned-out bunkhouse. At least no one died in there that I knew of. I did walk to the grave site and cried my eyes out. I looked at our house and cried some more. Every place I looked brought back fond memories. I'm so alone.

The next morning, I found an old shovel in the ruins of the bunkhouse and I went to the back side of the house. Mark and Jim had built an area where we could hide our gold and also a few guns and some ammo. It was like a rock safe with an iron top and it was buried about two feet below ground. I dug for what seemed like a week, but it was only a few hours. When I reach the safe, I was amazed at the amount of gold we had stored there. It was all from what Crow had stolen. Maybe that was the cause of everyone getting killed but me. It was my penance for what Crow had done. There was a Colt six-shooter and a holster and plenty of ammo. Also, there was somethings I had forgotten about, my Bowie knife and its sheaf and my grizzly bear claw necklace. The gold was in a saddlebag so it would be easy to carry. I stayed three days and nights at my old homestead and knew this would be the last time I'd come back here. I said some prayers and cried my eyes out again. I'm so down, so depressed and so lonely. I need the bitter shit and I need it now. I hurried back to Coulson and paid Vince off what I owed him. I then bought a small building down the street from the store for less than nothing. The town is becoming more deserted every day. I also bought a shit load of the bitter shit and I retired to my new home. I have a straw bed and one chair. There is sort of a kitchen, but I don't plan on eating. I just want to die and I'm almost there now.

Mildred, Vince's wife, came to my home and she was crying and very upset. I of course, was so relaxed from the bitter shit I could hardly understand what she was saying. It appeared that Vince was beaten to an inch of his life by some of the Young gang members. They wanted the gold from our property. It seems that they went back to the scene of their crimes searching for our stash of gold. They found the stone safe behind the house that I had left open and empty. They realized someone had found the safe and had taken their gold and they wanted it back. Vince told them nothing and they beat him badly. Doc Jones was with him now. Mildred asked me to go with her and see Vince.

I followed Mildred out of my house, and we walked to the store without saying another word to one another. Vince had a smile on his face, but his face was badly bruised. He said, "I never told them anything. They knew someone had been to your old homestead and found that safe. They wanted that gold. The big boy was a kid named Howard, that was the name of the kid that shot you wasn't it?"

Something inside of me moved me to be wide awake after I heard the name Howard. I smiled at Vince and said, "Howard, you say? He wanted our gold? The hell you say? Vince, I need to know where they are and how to find them, but first, I need to get myself straight."

Vince said, "He was planning on meeting with his uncles somewhere east of here. He said he'd be back in a month or so and I was supposed to have their gold here for them. He thinks I found the stash and I wanted it for myself. He'll give me month to have it for him. I couldn't give him a dime, we are broke. I'm closing up the store and moving to Billings. I just hope I'm not too late. Annie, if I were you, I'd just run away. Get out of here before they find out you're still alive."

I laughed and said, "That will not happen. A month you say? I'll need food, lots of food. Whatever you do, do not give me any of the bitter shit again, do you understand? I'm going to get myself right and then I'm going hunting. I'll be hunting for Young brothers' meat, if you get my meaning. Vince, you're a good friend and I'm going to give you and Mildred some of my gold. I will also tell you where the remainder of my stash will be in case, they kill me. You see Vince, I just don't give a shit if I live or die. This is the way I felt as a little girl when the Indians killed my family. When you feel as I do, you can commit any atrocity known to man and not feel any remorse. I will kill them all and then I'll walk away and find a new life."

CHAPTER THIRTY-FIVE

HOWARD

I took all of the bitter shit out to Vince's outhouse and I threw it down the hole. Even if I wanted that shit so badly, I'd have to draw the line about jumping in there to retrieve it. I began to eat, but I was still trying to wear off the effects of the bitter shit. I even began running up the mountain, but at first it was so very hard, I'm so weak. I also, began quick drawing again. I also shot the Winchester again and I am just an awful shot. I knew I'd get better; I needed that Winchester for longer range shooting, which I expected I'd need. You know, another thing, I was getting happier again. Happy to know I could do something to avenge my family's deaths. I knew I'd never find complete happiness again like I had in my life, I have just lost too much. It had been well over a year since my family was killed and even though it's been only a month since I got off the bitter shit, I feel stronger again.

I realize after three weeks of running every day, shooting every day and eating every day, I'm getting back to the old Annie. My quick draw is getting lighting quick again and I'm back being a dead eye with a Colt six-shooter. I'm still not where I want to be with that damn Winchester yet, but I'm hoping to get there soon. Vince has not left yet, and he comes by every day to watch me shoot. He also has watched me run up the mountainside and asks me why I'm doing that. I tell him in case someone chases me I can outrun them. Actually, I want to look better and feel better so I can get my old confidence back.

Several days after the month-long wait, Howard came into the empty store looking for Vince. He and Mildred had left by then and had moved to Billings. Howard had two gang members with him, and they were pissed off that Vince wasn't there. I saw them ride into town and I remained hidden in my little building. Howard and his two friends split up and walked around town knocking at all the doors of the empty buildings. I figured the best way to take on these idiots was one at a time, with Howard being the last. I had a special treatment for him.

I waited in my little building and left the door wide open with several gold coins resting on my little table. A dirty older man knocked at the open door and saw the coins. He walked in and started to pick up the coins when I stepped out and said, "May I ask what you're doing in my home? Those are also my gold coins, which I found up the mountain at a burned-out homestead."

The man smiled and said, "Did you find more than just these? Oh my, you are a real cutie, how about you and I having some fun here today?"

I replied, "Yeah, I'd like that very much. I haven't had sex since some men killed my husband about a year ago. Do you want to do it right here or go somewhere else? And if you are with some friends, please don't tell them what we're going to do here. I don't want anyone to think I'm a whore."

"Why don't we just do it here and I promise I won't tell my friends." He began to take off his gun belt when I walked close to him. He was smiling ear to ear, when I quickly shoved the blade of my Bowie knife under his chin and up and into his mouth. His mouth opened and I could see the blade of my knife had pierced through his tongue and had gone up and through the roof of his mouth. He had a frightened, panic look on his face as he struggled to remove the knife from his mouth. He was gagging and choking and making muttering sounds.

I said, "Isn't this better than sex? Now, you'll know how it feels like to have someone take advantage of you. You fucked with the wrong woman today, you sorry excuse for a man."

He was trying to grab his gun from his holster that wasn't there any longer, he had forgotten he took it off and it was laying on the floor. He grabbed the handle of my knife with both hands still trying to pull it out of his mouth all the while I was laughing at him. It was quite funny. He finally dropped dead onto the ground and I stepped on his face and removed my knife. I walked around to the back of the building and began waiting for another victim. One down and two to go. This was getting to be fun.

I saw Howard across the road walking door to door, but I didn't see the other guy. Just then the other man came around the building and almost bumped into me. He was very apologetic and kept saying he was so sorry. He asked, "What is a fine young woman like you doing here in this godforsaken ghost town?"

I answered, "I'm looking for a couple of men that killed my family, you wouldn't know anything about that would you?"

The man was perplexed, he looked at me with a confused look on his face. He said, "Someone killed your family? I don't know anything about that. I heard some folks died around here a year ago or so, but they were killers and thieves."

He began to draw his six-shooter out of his holster, but I cleared leather long before he could. I shot him in his mouth. He reached for his face and I then pulled his revolver out of his holster. He couldn't cry or talk he just held onto his jaw that was hanging down into his hands. He sank to the floor and I walked away. I knew Howard would hear the shot and would come a running.

Howard ran into the back of the building and saw his buddy. He screamed, "Freddy, what in the hell happened to you? What happened?" Freddy, however, couldn't talk with his jaw hanging down into his hands.

That's when I stepped out and into the open and shot Howard in the right kneecap. He fell to the ground screaming in pain. He reached for his gun and I shot off the other kneecap. As he was rolling around on the ground, I stepped on the first knee I had shot and said, "Don't you move again, if you do, I'll blow a hole in that stupid face of yours large enough that a rat will be able to climb through." He stopped moving and I reached down and took his revolver from his holster. I then said, "You don't remember me do ya?"

"Why should I remember a bitch like you. You don't know who you're screwing with, you are dead meat. Do you hear me, dead meat?"

I sat on my haunches and I had my Bowie knife in my right hand. Howard couldn't see it and I played with him a bit. I said, "Howie, Howie, I remember you. You were the one that said you weren't stupid, and your uncles weren't stupid either, but you all are. You are so stupid." I then drove the blade of my Bowie knife into the back of his hand that was supporting his body. The look on his face as he was falling backward said it all, he now remembered, and he knew he was a dead man.

As I pulled the Bowie knife out of his hand, I saw his friend reaching for me. I then shoved the knife deep into his groin area. That stopped him immediately. He muttered in pain. I finished him off with a shot to the head.

I then said to Howie, "You will not get off so lucky as your friend Freddy here. You are gonna suffer for what you did. You should have made sure you killed me you stupid fool. When I'm done with you, you will tell me exactly where I can find Spike and Foxy."

Howie was breathing hard; he was in so much pain but was trying to hide it. He said, "You'll get nothing from me. And I really enjoyed shooting those kids. You should have heard all the crying that was coming for that house after we dynamited it. Crying, crying and more crying."

I then drove my Bowie knife deep into his right thigh. I pulled it out and then drove it into his left thigh. He didn't think that was very funny. I asked, "Where are your uncles? If you tell me, I'll get this over with quicker and it will be less painful."

"Fuck you bitch!"

The Bowie now was shoved into his right armpit. It came out as quick as it went in and then into the other armpit. It must have hurt because poor Howie began to cry. He tearfully said, "Okay, okay, I'll tell you. They are staying in a place called Settlers Gulch. It's a one-horse town east of here. Foxy has a woman there and Spike likes the place because there is gambling, and all the players are pigeons. By pigeons I mean easy pickings. Will you please stop the torture now? I've had enough."

I said, "Well Howie, that was very kind of you to tell me where I can find your family members so I can kill them, as you killed mine. But if you think the torture is over, you are sadly mistaken, it's just begun."

I worked on Howie for over an hour longer but not with the Bowie knife. I just sat and tormented him with my words. He continued to scream even though I was done with him physically. I left him alive so he could pray to God for His forgiveness. I thought about what my family members went through at the hands of this man Howard Young. '*My little daughter Katie who would never experience life as an adult. Addie-Lou who was experiencing her first love, and her life was taken so easily by these men. And Walk and She, just young women that had been abused by these Young brothers. They never experienced life or love. And little Hawk, finding his first love too and was killed along side of her. Poor Mary who was just looking for someone to love her. Jim and Maggie, died with their children, what parent would want to see or do that. The love of my life, my husband Mark. The best husband and father ever. And Manda. She was such a good friend and she helped me so when I was young. I miss them all so. My God, I can't seem to get them out of my mind. The bitter shit used to help but now without it, I don't know what I'll do. I know I'm dying inside; I'm so messed up. Will the pain ever go away? I guess not.'*

I then headed to Settlers Gulch to find the Young brothers. I'm in deep thought, *'Maybe I'm trying to find something else. Maybe closure, or maybe my death, only time will tell.'*

CHAPTER THIRTY-SIX

FINDING LORI

The Gulch as I've always called it, is several days ride away. I'm not in a hurry for I now believe my death is imminent. I don't care, there is nothing left for me to live for. I will take out my vengeance on these men and I will be willing to give up my life to do so.

As I rode towards the Gulch, I made the decision to go back and see our old homestead. There are memories there that might help me forget the sadness and despair I feel. What do I care how the place looks like now? I always said I'd never go back but something is driving me back. Maybe it's Mom. I guess she wants me to say some prayers for her. I can do that.

The ride up the hillside brings back memories of my first ride up there with Crow. I was so worried but when we reached the top of the hill, even though Old Ned farted all the way up, I was astounded by the beauty of the place. I remember seeing the cabin for the first time and how wonderful it was. My own bedroom and two dogs, Moon and Shine. I thought if there was a heaven on earth, this was it.

When I reached the top of the hill, I got a very big surprise, the place was beautiful again. The cabin was restored but the old barn was gone. In its place was a smaller barn and a corral. There was also a new outhouse, but it was much closer to the cabin, where a person such as me could use it at nighttime. There were gardens on both sides of the yard and all the old bushes and brush had been cleared. As I sat on my horse looking around, the door opened, and a very large dog ran out to greet me. He didn't bark or growl, he just wiggled up to me. I jumped off my horse and began to scratch him behind his ears. He was a mix of, I think, wolf and some breed of dog. Following behind him was a cute, dirty, little girl. She had long black hair, brown eyes, freckles galore and big dimples in both cheeks. She was maybe seven or eight years old and was so happy to see me. She didn't stop when she reached me, she jumped into my arms and squeezed me very hard, she had tears in her eyes and said, "Hi, I'm Lori and this is my pooch Ronnie. We named him after a neighbor Mr. Naslund back in Minnesota. I knew you'd come. What's your name? You are going to stay with me? Please don't leave me."

I smiled at the chatty little Lori and said, "Hi, I'm Annie and I lost my dogs that I used to have when I lived here. I lived here when I was a little girl like you. Who do you live here with?"

She grabbed my hand and said, "Come with me and we can go into the cabin and lock the door and talk."

I tied up my horse to a small post and followed Lori into the cabin. She immediately bolted the door. There was no one in there and I was a bit confused. Who would leave a little girl like this by herself? I then thought, *'Crow would have. In fact, he did that all the time. I did, however, have two large dogs or a couple of wolves to protect me.'*

Lori said after we entered, "Would you like something to drink?"

I replied, "No Lori, but thanks for asking. Now, who do you live with?"

Lori made a big sigh before saying, "I live here now by myself. Mommy and Daddy hid me in the woods before it happened. Some very bad men shot Daddy and Mommy to death. I stayed in the woods for three days with Ronnie. When the men were leaving with Mommy, she jumped out of the wagon and started running to me in the woods. They shot her in the back. I saw the whole thing from my hiding place.

They took Mommy and Daddy's bodies with them and just left. There were five of them in all. I've been waiting here for someone to come and help me. There is a hiding place in the cabin where I can go if some men were to show up. But I saw it was you and I wasn't worried, so I didn't hide."

I had tears running down my cheeks as she was telling me her story. What in the hell is wrong with these men? Have they all been brought up to take what they want and leave everyone dead? I grabbed my new little friend and hugged her, and I said, "I'll take care of you, don't you worry anymore. How have you been getting food? Has Ronnie been foraging for food?"

Lori smiled and said, "I knew God would send me someone. I just knew it. Mommy always told me to pray when I needed something, and God would always take care of me. She said sometimes it might take Him awhile to get to my request because He is so busy helping others, but He will always provide for me. It did take Him quite a while this time to get you to come and find me, but here you are. I am hungry, I've been eating just apples from our tree and Mommy had some jars of vegetables and other fruit stored in our hideout. Those bad men that killed Mommy and Daddy ate all our other food."

"Lori, I have some jerky in my saddlebags, I'll go and get it. After you eat, we're going hunting, so you can have a real meal tonight. I see your folks had planted some potatoes, some beans and peas. We'll have us a feast. And you, young lady, are going to take a bath in the creek over there."

I took Lori down to the creek where I used to bathe, and we took off our clothes and jumped in. She is the sweetest little girl. She reminds me of Addie-Lou and Katie. Thinking of them brings tears to my eyes. Lori looks at me as says, "Annie, why are you crying? Aren't you having fun anymore?"

I hugged her again and said, "Being with you brings back memories of my children. They're both dead and seeing you jumping around and having fun reminds me of the times they did that. I'm really alright, finding you has made me very happy. I'm not going to let anything happen to you, I promise."

Little Lori laughed, and said, "God brought you to me, so I know you'll take care of me. Can we live in my cabin?"

"Lori, I have to do something before I can come back and live with you, but I will be back. First off, I'll need to get you some food and make sure the cabin is secure. I'll be gone for a few days. Will that be all right?"

"I wish you didn't have to leave me. Could I come with you?"

"Oh sweetie, I just can't have you come along this time. There some very bad men I need to see. They might be the ones that killed your mom and dad."

CHAPTER THIRTY-SEVEN

REVENGE IS SO SWEET

I've been with my new little friend Lori Jones, for about three months now. I can't believe God sent her to me. That's what Lori always says, and I agree. She is about the cutest little bugger I've ever seen and what a personality. My mom used to say that a person with that kind of spunk was 'full of piss and vinegar.' I'm not sure what that means, but I'm sure it was a compliment, since that's what she said about me. I take Lori every place I go. I will not leave her alone and she doesn't want to be left alone. We've hunted for fowl, rabbits but no squirrel, we both hate the taste of squirrel meat. We also shot a deer and Lori didn't like gutting it. I told her she'd have to learn, and I made her help. After she said, "Damn, that was hard to do. But I did it, didn't I?"

I said, "What's with using the swear word, damn?"

She replied, "You say it all the time, why can't I?"

I hugged her tight and said, "You can say whatever you want when it's just to two of us around. But when you meet others or you have a boyfriend, you must be ladylike all the time and ladies don't swear. Except for me."

My little bugger smiled and said, "Can I say the word fuck too, when we're alone?"

I was surprised, and I said, "Where in the world did you hear that word, it wasn't from me?"

"I heard it from Daddy many times. Especially when he was building that damn barn and that damn outhouse. He used to say the word fuck whenever something didn't go right, which was often. When I say often, I mean all the time, every day. Mommy just told me to ignore it, but it was hard to do. I also heard those awful men that killed Mommy and Daddy say it. And they said it in almost every sentence."

"Okay, lets you and I make a pact, we'll never say that word again as long as we live. Can you accept that? How about a pinky swear?"

Lori looked at me very confused and asked, "What's a pinky swear? And why are you holding up your little finger?"

I said, "You've never heard of a pinky swear? Well, your little finger is called a pinky finger. And, in a place, far, far way called Japan, they started the ritual. They interlock their pinky fingers and make a promise that can never be broken. My mom told me about it, and I made a couple of promises using my pinky finger. One was with my husband Mark when we got married. Oh Lori, I loved him so."

"Okay, let's make a pinky swear that we won't ever say the word fuck again. Oops, sorry about that, it won't happen again." As she was beginning to laugh so hard, I grabbed that little shit and I began tickling her until she said, "Stop, I'm going to pee my pants!" I stopped but I chased her all the way to the outhouse. She's so much fun.

I'm still planning on going after the Young boys, but I just can't leave Lori alone right now. Lori also has some lingering thoughts about her mom and dad's deaths. Sometimes in the middle of the night she crawls in bed with me and cuddles up real close. I never say anything to her, I just hug her back and she falls back asleep. She frequently asks me why her mom wasn't killed right away? I just say I don't know. I also say her mom probably stayed alive so she could pray for those bad men. This poor little kid, she is so sad sometimes but snaps out of it as soon as I tease her. I know it will take some time for her to get over it but she's on her way now. It took me a very long time too, but I did have Crow and Mom.

I asked Lori if she wanted to go hunting with me. I wanted to shoot a couple of pheasants and maybe a goose or two. They all are good eating and Lori said her mouth was watering just thinking about it. We closed up the house and I found an old padlock that Lori's dad had, and I locked our home up. I always wore my holstered six-shooter and I brought along an old shotgun I found in the barn. Lori said her dad used it to shoot fowl. He said they were easier to shoot with a shotgun rather than Winchester or some other kind of rifle. I never shot a gun like this before, but I was eager to try. There were lots of shells in a box and I told Lori, "Let's take the box with us. I may want to target practice."

We walked into the woods and I remembered all that we had done in those woods. I also thought about the dead bodies we carried out there to rot. So many bad memories but so many good ones too.

We were deep in the woods when our dog Ronnie began to growl something fierce. I told Lori to stand still and I motioned with my hand for Ronnie to be quiet. There in the clearing ahead was a big ass grizz and he was looking directly at us. I knew if he attacked, we were all dead meat. All I could think about was shooting this antiquated shotgun with the two barrels at him. For the grizz it would be like swatting mosquitoes, nothing more. He stood on his hind legs and sniffed into the air. I whispered to Lori, "If he charges, you run as fast as you can the other way. I'll unload the shotgun first and then my six-shooter. You leave Ronnie here with me. Okay?"

Lori just shook her head no. She said, "If you die, then so will I. I'm not going to be alone again. Please don't make me do that Mommy."

The little shit called me Mommy. Mommy! I smiled at her and said, "Don't you run if he charges, we'll die together but we'll die fighting."

All of sudden, Ronnie bolted straight at the grizz barking and growling. The grizz turned tail and ran deep into the forest with Ronnie chasing him. I yelled, "Ronnie you sweet pooch, get your ass back here."

I then heard my daughter laugh and yell, "Ronnie, get your ass back here." Ronnie came running back wagging his tail. Lori and I both knelt down and praised and scratched him. He saved our lives. We need more dogs.

As Lori, Ronnie and I were walking back from our fruitless hunt, we heard some commotion coming from our homestead. At first, I thought it was the grizz, but after a short spell I could tell it was humans. I stopped in my tracks as did Lori. I walked back a few steps and told Ronnie to sit and stay. Lori tugged at my shirt and after I looked down at her she said, "Those are two of the men that hurt Mommy and Daddy."

I grabbed her by her hand and I said, "Come with me." Lori and I walked quite a ways away from the homestead. I had her sit on a log near a stand of trees and said, "Lori, I want you to stay here and don't move. Ronnie will stay with you. These are the same men I was looking for. If you wait here for me to return, I can take care of them for what they did to your family." She smiled and shook her head up and down for yes.

I slowly walked towards the cabin and I realized that there were only two of them. They were trying ferociously to get the lock off the door. I walked up behind them, about fifteen to twenty paces away. I laughed out loud and when they heard me, they turned and were very surprised. One was the coward Foxy and the other was just part of their gang. I said, "Are you boys trying to rob my cabin?"

Foxy looked at me with a confused look on his face and said, "Who are you? You look like a bitch we killed a while back. Whatcha call yourself?"

I was so ready for this. I knew these two idiots were so slow drawing a six-shooter, so I teased them a bit before I shot um. I said, "The name's Annie Crow. No one has killed me lately. Some have tried, but they were all too stupid to succeed." After hearing my name and my stupid comment, a look of fright appeared on Foxie's face. The other guy just looked like the dumb shit he was. I whispered, "Go for it Foxy and enjoy your last breath." It was no contest, I shot Foxy in his chest and the other idiot directly in the heart. I knew I shouldn't torture them with Lori around, so I quietly said to Foxy, "Does that hurt?" I was looking at his chest. "If it does, I can put you out of your misery, would you like that?"

He gritted his teeth and said, "Fuck you, bitch! There ain't nuttin more you can do to me. And I'll get ya. If I don't my brother and our gang will."

"Foxy, Foxy! We don't use the word fuck around here. It's against our rules." I shot him at close range right in his groin. He passed out immediately. I walked slowly over to the other idiot and took his gun. I looked it over and I realized it was my husband Mark's military pistol. I was so angry I was shaking. I fired four rounds into the idiot's dead body. I then returned to Foxy. He was coming to but in extreme pain. I quietly said, "Foxy, how does it feel to be like a woman, you know, ball-less?"

"Finish me, finish me! I can't take this anymore. Please?"

I said, "No can do! You're going home on horseback, which I hope is very painful." I dragged what was left of his body and I strapped him onto the saddle on his horse. I tied his hands with a rope, and I extended the rope around the horse's belly and tied the rope to his legs very tight. I then wound the rope through the stirrups and up around the saddle horn, which would prevent the body from falling off the horse. I did the same to the dead idiot. It was hard work getting those two lying across their saddles, but I wanted to send a message to Spike.

I then swatted their horses, and they took off running for home. I was hoping it was straight to Spike.

I quickly walked to where my daughter Lori was waiting for me. She jumped off the log and hugged me. She said, "Did ya get um. I hope so?"

"Yeah, I got um good. Now, you and I and our furry mutt here are going to have to live in the woods for a while, are you okay with that?"

"Whoopee. I'd love to stay in the forest with you Mom. Are we gonna sleep out here too? I didn't like sleeping here when those men attacked us. I know I will if I'm with you. You'll protect me."

"Yes, I will. But the reason I want to stay in the forest, is to surprise those bad men that will be looking for us. Now, they won't know who sent their friends back to them, so I want to surprise them. And what better way to surprise them than to hide in the forest. I think we'll be able to hide so they can't find us, and we'll be able to pick them off one by one with the Winchester."

CHAPTER THIRTY-EIGHT

THE LAST ATTACK

We stayed in the cabin for the first two nights, then we moved into the woods. We brought food and water with us and we felt free to move around until late afternoons. It was going on a week when they arrived in the late morning. I had strategically hidden two Winchester rifles and shells within fifty yards of one another about a hundred yards away from the cabin. I also placed a six-shooter alongside of the Winchesters. There was plenty of cover. I also had the shotgun with me and Lori, as well as Mark's military pistol. I thought it would be apropos to shoot one of these men in the head with the pistol, like they did to my Mark.

I told Lori it was time that she and Ronnie were to go deep into the woods. She replied, "Yes Mommy, but you be careful. God does not want you to leave me, so don't you dare let anything happen to you."

"I won't. I love you little lady."

"I love you too Mom."

As I was crawling to my first weapon site I thought, *'I'm so lucky having her in my life after losing my entire family twice. I better be careful. I know these men are ruthless killers, but they are cowards and they all lack expertise with guns. They can shoot close up but not from long range or quick drawing. I definitely have the advantage.'*

As I put the Winchester to my shoulder and looked straight ahead, there was Spike standing near the door to the cabin. Looking them over I counted five in all. I'm clearly outnumbered. I wonder if there were some more of them down the hill. There could be. If so, I needed to shoot as many as possible and head for Lori and move deep into the woods. My first shot would be at Spike. I aimed at his head and I fired my Winchester. I missed! His big head moved as I pulled the trigger, but I still made a hit to his upper chest. He dropped like a wounded deer, and he was screaming and grasping like a little girl. It appeared that he was in excruciating pain. Good! His buddies left him and headed for cover. I was going to try and get to my other location, but before leaving, I realized I had a perfect shot at another one of the gunmen. I fired two shots in secession, and I hit him in his head with both shots and I saw him roll around on the ground. All of a sudden, I was hearing bullets pinging and zinging all around me, the guys that were left were all good shots. I had underestimated them. I had to duck for cover to dodge all of the shots aimed at me. I began to crawl away from all the activity. I got further back in the woods and found my other Winchester. I rested my rifle against a tree stump and found my target. It was one of the guys that I'm sure had killed my family members. I sighted him in and pulled the trigger, and I saw him jerk backwards. I think I may have killed him, but I was not sure.

After my last shot, I saw someone make a slow dash to a horse. It was clearly Spike trying to mount his horse. I aimed at him and missed. I had inadvertently shot his horse in the neck and it bucked once and fell over with Spike still holding on for dear life. He was pinned below it and yelling for help. I thought, *'I think two are dead and Spike is pinned below his horse. Two more should be still alive, if I counted correctly. I need to move around and dodge the bullets, or I'll die here.'*

I began to crawl again to find more cover. The shooting stopped temporarily. Spike's friends were trying to help him get the horse off his legs. One of the men, grabbed a hold of Spike and tried to pull him out from under the horse. I stopped my crawl and realized I had a clear shot at the guy that was trying to help Spike. I aimed my Winchester and pulled the trigger. The shot had so much force, my target was slammed backwards about ten feet in the air. It was after that when I heard loud bang close to me and I felt the excruciating pain in my left arm as I dropped to the ground. I then heard a man yell, "I got the bitch, I got the bitch! Spike, I got the bitch, what do you want me to do now?"

Spike's voice was very weak and he quietly said, "Are you sure? If you got her, let's get the hell out of here. This was not worth losing three of our guys over this stupid bitch. Get over here and help get this horse off of me."

As the man got up and began to walk towards Spike, I stood up and drew my Colt out of my holster and yelled, "Sorry boys but I'm still alive." I then unloaded my Colt into his buddy, all in his gut. It was a very good shooting since I was about fifty feet away. He was clearly dead.

Four of them were dead, but Spike was still stuck below his dead horse. I walked slowly over to him and pointed my empty Colt at him. I said, "Spike, where's your six-shooter? If you have it in your hand you are going to die a very painful death."

Spike lifted his six-shooter over his head holding the barrel. Even though I was in a lot of pain, I managed to take the revolver away from him. It was a Colt and I'm sure it was one of my family's weapons. I pulled out my Bowie knife with my good arm and showed it to him. I'm sure after seeing my knife he knew I meant business. He looked up at me and said, "You're dead, I saw your body. You can't be alive; you just can't be alive."

"No, I'm not alive Spike, I'm a ghost. I came back to kill you and that stupid nephew of yours, young Howie. He killed my husband and my daughter, and you killed my other daughter and the rest of my family members. So, with that being said, you are going to suffer. You may think you've suffered enough already, but you haven't."

"Please, I'm sorry, it wasn't my idea, it was Foxy. He wanted to get even with you for killing Roger. You know he was crazy? You know that?"

I had the Bowie knife in my hand, and I turned the blade around and around so Spike could see how big the blade was. I held it close to his face to make sure he could see it. As I said before he was close to being blind. He said, "Please let me go, I'll never, ever bother you again, I promise."

I replied, "I know you won't bother me again." I drove the blade deep into his chest. I wiggled it around a bit before pulling it out. He made no sounds as the blood squirted out from the wound. I slit his throat just in case he was still alive. I checked to make sure they were all dead and they were. I yelled for Lori to come and help me. She came out and looked at the bodies and said nothing.

I asked her, "Are you alright?"

She smiled and said, "Mom, I couldn't be better. It was all very scary but thanks for doing this and please don't ever think this will bother me, because it won't. I just wish I was older so I could have helped you. I want you to teach me how to shoot like you. Mom, you're hurt! Did you get shot?"

I said, "You're right honey, I got shot. I'll need you to help me stop the bleeding. I think the bullet went in one side and out the other. We just need to stop the bleeding. I'll show you how."

My little Lori is so tough. I told her about cauterizing a wound and she went right ahead and did it without blinking an eye. I think all she's gone through in her short life has prepared her for this type of things happening. My little girl is something very special.

CHAPTER THIRTY-NINE

THE GULCH

It took us several days to drag the killers away from our home. Instead of dragging them into the woods, Lori had a better idea. She thought it would be easier if we just dragged them down our hill and out to the prairie. I agreed. It took longer but we got their bodies a longer distance away from our homestead. After we left the first two bodies, we looked back, and the vultures were circling in the air already looking for a place to land. We stopped to watch what was happening. Coyotes, fox and other varmints were milling around looking for a place to attack for a good meal. We'd need to drop the next bodies further away.

After completing the job of ridding ourselves of the bodies, we then worked on cleaning up the yard and the area where the men died. My arm was feeling a bit better, but it was still very sore.

After a couple of months had passed, I realized we now have five additional horses to feed and we don't have enough feed for all of them. We need to sell at least four of them. So, the only place to go is back to Settlers Gulch. I asked Lori if she would mind if I left her alone and she emphatically said, "No! Please don't leave me, I don't ever want you to leave me alone again. Please Mommy, don't leave me!"

Whenever she uses the word Mommy it just breaks me up. The little shit knows how to work me. I do understand her not wanting to be left alone again, but the Gulch is no place for a little girl. I guess it doesn't matter, I just can't leave her. Besides, we need food and clothing and I'll need her with me to get somethings that will fit her. She's got so little clothing left, but then again so do I. I've got to check my gold supply, I maybe running short. We found nothing on the losers I killed. No wonder they came after me, they thought I was rich. Ha, ha!

We mounted our horses and had ropes around the four horses we're going to sell. Lori was so excited. She said she couldn't remember ever being in a town. In fact, she said she didn't remember seeing anyone before the bad men rode into her homestead. I told her the last time I was in Settler Gulch it was a pretty bad place, and I was forced to defend myself. She didn't care, she wanted to see and meet other people and maybe someone her age.

It took a day and half to get to the Gulch, caring for four additional horses was a big job. As we entered what I will now refer to as a town and it was an unbelievable town now. There were many wooden structures and men, and women were walking around with no fear. The women were mostly all wearing fashionable clothing, you know nice dresses, and some were wearing fancy hats. There were still some cowboys wandering around and they were still toting six-guns but not in a threatening manner. Next to Gorman's store was the marshal's office. I laughed and thought, *'Law and order had come to the Gulch. New houses and new businesses. Gorman had expanded his store, it was immense.'* We first dropped off the horses that we wanted to sell at the livery stable and we were told we'd get eight dollars in gold apiece for them. That was a nice profit of thirty-six dollars. I said to my daughter Lori, "Follow me, we're going shopping." Lori was all smiles. She grabbed my hand and we walked towards Gorman's store.

We walked into the store and it was crowded with shoppers. The place was huge, when I say huge, I mean immense, or just damn right big. As Lori and I were walking around a familiar looking man walked towards us and said with a smile on his face, "Welcome strangers, and top of the morning to you. I'm Mike Gorman and I own this establishment, what can I do for you lovely ladies?"

He didn't recognize me, which I thought was good. I said, "We're looking for some dresses and some work clothes and some unmentionables'"

Mr. Gorman laughed and said, "Unmentionables? Do you mean underwear? If so, we have a lot of unmentionables. They're right over here in our women's sections. You'll also find every other garment there too. If you need assistance, I'd be glad to help or if you need a woman's touch, I'll send Betty over."

I smiled at him and said, "I think we'll be just fine helping ourselves. But thank you Mr. Gorman."

Gorman stared at me for a second or two and smiled. He said, "I thought I recognized you? You're Annie Crow? Annie, don't you remember me, I sure as hell remember you?"

I replied, "Why yes Mr. Gorman, I remember you. It was quite a while ago now, but I remember you. It would appear business is booming, and I also see there is a marshal's office here now. Law and order, I never thought this would happen. This is my daughter Lori."

Lori crept behind me and waved at Gorman. I realized she was a little shy. This little shit is shy, my outgoing little girl is shy.

Gorman said, "Lori, if you'd like, Betty over by the counter has some candy I think you might like. I'd like to talk to your mom for a bit." Gorman asked Betty to assist Lori.

After Lori walked away, Gorman said, "I remember you so well. You took care of that man in front of my store that accosted you. You were with an Indian kid; I think his name was Wind. Well, you were both just kids. All the old town folks know of you and talk about you often. You are a real hero around here. The stories I'm sure have been embellished a bit now-a-days, but I watched you in action. I also heard about somethings that happened outside of Coulson, as well as in the town too. Someone said you were killed by the Young brothers, but you rose from the dead and killed all of them. Is any of that true?"

"Wow, you have heard a lot of shit about me. Some is true and some is not. I didn't die, but they thought I did. And yes, I killed all of those Young boys, the last of them just a few months ago. They were killers and they deserved to die. They massacred my entire family. They also killed my little daughter Lori's family too."

"Annie, there are a few people I'd like you to meet here in town. The one for sure is our new marshal. He's new to this area and he's told me he's heard about you. He's a very nice man and a very fair man. When I say a fair man, I mean he's fair in understanding and settling disputes. His name is Marshal Patrick Mountain."

I asked "Is Marshal Mountain an Indian? With name of Mountain, I'm guessing he's an Indian?"

Gorman smiled and said, "No, he's not Indian but I think he said he's Irish. He's a good-looking guy and very nice. All the single women in town are after him. But I think a self-sufficient woman like yourself would be more to his liking."

"I'm not interested in any man now or in the future. I lost my man and I'm not looking for a replacement. I have a child to care for and that is my main concern now-a-days."

"Please let me take you next door to just meet him. I'm sure he has some questions regarding those Young boys he'd like to ask you. He also wanted to meet you if you ever came back into town."

I told Lori to come with us, but she asked if she could stay with Betty. She loved the candy and wanted to look at the clothes. I guess she's becoming a shopper.

Mr. Gorman and I walked next door and into the marshal's office and there sat a handsome young man. Mr. Gorman was right; he was handsome and built too. He got up from his chair as soon as we walked in and strolled directly towards me. He put out his hand and I shook it. He looked directly into my eyes and said, "Please come in and sit down."

Gorman said, "Pat, this here is Annie Crow, I'm sure you've heard about her."

Pat said, "I knew it was you Annie, I was told you were a beauty and you certainly are. It is so nice to meet a strong, beautiful woman such as you."

I replied, "Wow, I don't ever recall being called a strong, beautiful woman before. Most men in years past called me a whore or a slut or just a killer. But thank you Marshal Mountain, that was a nice compliment."

"Please, just call me Pat, I hate all that formal bullshit. Sorry, I didn't mean to swear in front of you, it's just that I'm always with just men. This is a nice change for me."

Gorman excused himself and said he had to get back to work. He said he'd watch over Lori for me. I thanked him and before saying to Pat, "How long have you been a marshal here in the Gulch?"

"I've been here for about eight months, but I've been in law enforcement for almost ten years."

"So, you've heard of me, what exactly have you heard?"

"I've heard you are the first woman here in the west that is not afraid of a man with a gun. And you can outdraw most any man alive. I've also heard you've lost your entire family at the hands of the Young brothers. I also heard now that you may have killed all of them. You have a reputation around here, but I'm sure you don't know that in the entire west you are a person not to be trifled with. Lawmen in particular have a high regard for you. You've helped clean up this area of a lot of lawlessness. So, that's what I heard about you. What do you say?"

I replied, "I'm stunned. No one has ever told me any of that crap. But Mr. Mountain, I thank you for the kind words. I must be going."

Pat shook his head and said, "I see you wear a grizzly claw around your neck, did you kill a grizz?"

"Why yes, I did, but it was years ago, I think I was about fourteen or so then."

"Holy shit, fourteen years old. Not many fifty-year-old men can say they slayed a grizz."

"I must be going Mr. Mountain."

"Please don't leave until I've finished. Would it be possible to come and visit you at your homestead? I promise my intentions are good. It's just that I like you and respect you. I'd like to get to know you better."

"Are you kidding? Why would you want to get to know me better? You already know I'm a loose cannon. Like everyone around here says, I killed for the fun of it. If they only knew what my life has been like. It's been pretty rough and now I have a daughter back that I lost and I'm going to hopefully live a quiet life."

Pat again smiled and said, "That's what I'm hoping to do too, live a quiet life. So, with all that being said, can I visit you?"

"You want to come and visit my daughter and me at our homestead? Alright, it's okay with me but I warn you, you better behave."

Pat asked, "Would it be alright if I brought my kids? I have a boy and a girl; they're twins and are eight years old."

I was kind of shocked, I asked, "Where's your wife, wouldn't she care if you came for a visit?"

"My wife passed on five years ago. She came down with some sort of cough and never got better. She died about a month after contacting that disease. So, with that being said, could I bring my kids?"

"I'd love for you and your family to come for a visit. Let me draw you a map." After I drew the map, I went back to the store. After I found Lori looking at dresses someone tapped me on my shoulder, it was Pat again.

Pat said, "I wanted to meet you daughter. Hi, I'm Pat, what's your name?"

Lori remained very quiet until I said, "Lori, tell Pat what your name is and how old you are, he has kids about your age. They are coming to our place for a visit."

That was all it took; my little Lori became a chatterbox. She told Pat her name and age. She wanted to know all about his kids, were they boys or girls? How old were they, what were their names, and could they stay for more than a day?"

Pat replied, "They're twins, a boy and a girl. Their names Bill and Rose. And if your mom says it's okay, we'll stay a little longer. But if you two get sick of us, we'll leave right away."

Pat said he'd be at our homestead within a week. He needed to tie up a few things before taking some time off. Lori and I said we were looking forward to seeing him and his kids.

Lori and I finished our shopping and rode out of town. It was then that Lori said something that would change our lives.

CHAPTER FORTY

GOLD

As Lori and I were riding home, and after talking about Pat and his family coming for a visit, I told her I was worried about our financial future. I had finally looked at our gold supply and it had dwindled substantially. In fact, there were only a few nuggets of gold left. I told her I was worried that we wouldn't have enough to live on. She quickly said, "Mom, I have some nuggets stored in the barn. I guess I forgot all about them. Daddy showed me where he kept them. He was always panning for gold in our creek. I think there's still some gold in that creek. Mommy used to yell at him for spending so much time in that damn creek, as she called it. She wanted him to work in the gardens and cut firewood for winter. They both laughed with each other about what was most important, food, shelter or gold. Food and shelter always won out."

I thought to myself, *'Gold in that old creek? If Crow had known that, he'd have been in that damn creek day and night. Wind would have been in it every hour of the day too. Maybe I would have been too?'*

I said to little Lori, "Do you know where in the creek your dad found gold?"

She replied, "Why of course I do, I helped him all the time. I didn't have anyone to play with so I would wade out in our creek and help Daddy. It's easy to find the gold. Mommy called the gold shit; she didn't like it. She always said, 'If you can't eat it, it's shit.' She also called it 'man's downfall. No good comes from gold,' she used to say. That's the only thing they fought about, was gold."

When we arrived back at our homestead, we put our new clothes in the cabin and walked to the barn. Lori walked to the back of the small barn and lifted up a pile of small rocks and dug out a pretty large leather bag. She said, "Mom, help me."

I lifted out the bag and it was full of gold nuggets. Now, they were not large nuggets but smaller ones but nonetheless it was gold. I had no idea of their value, but it had to be substantial. I told her that we now had enough to live on, but I wanted to try and find some more.

I was always curious how her dad could have built that barn by himself, so I asked her, and she said, "Daddy had help in building our barn. And he had help building our new outhouse and shoring up the cabin. The wood and the logs were all there from the old barn and the old outhouse. Three men and two women that called themselves Negros, helped Daddy for over two whole years. They were very nice, and they said they were from the south, wherever that is. They also told stories about being slaves. They left the south after what they called the civil war that gave them their freedom. They were heading further west to find a place to live where no one would bother them. The men's names were Abe, Homer and July. The lady's names were Venus and Ruth."

I asked, "How did they come to help your folks out?"

"They showed up one day when Daddy was trying to rebuild that barn. Mom said they were a mess. They were dirty and hungry, and Abe and July had been beaten up by some white boys that wanted their women. They asked my folks if they could stay if they all helped out building the barn. My folks told me at first, they were skeptical of them, but they soon found out they were good people. The first week Dad made them sleep outside, but after a short while they came in and slept in the house. It was crowded but it was fun, they were all so nice. After Dad got to know them and saw how hard they all worked he began to trust them more. In fact, Dad showed them how to pan for gold. Every evening after they worked all day, Dad and the boys all panned for gold. When all the work was done, they had enough gold to buy horses and a wagon. Dad had to buy those things for them since no one would sell anything to Negros. Dad also found a bunch of old rifles in the ruins of the old barn, so they fixed them all up and took them along with them. They sadly left us a few years ago. Dad and Mom liked all of them so much, but it was time for them to leave. They now had enough gold for a good start in life."

I laughed at the comment about the old rifles. I told Lori, "Those old rifles were from my dad Crow. He had so many old guns in that barn, that we just took the best ones with us when we left. They must have found the stash. Good for them. It sure sounds like they were good people. I've never seen or met a Negro before, and I didn't know they were out here in the west. So that's how this place got all fixed up. When I first saw it, I couldn't believe it was the same place I had left."

"I'm glad you like it and want to stay with me."

"Lori, I'd never leave you. I'm here for good. If we move it will be together. So now let's you and I get rich. Let's pan for gold."

Lori knew just how to do the panning, I didn't. We worked the spots she suggested and luckily, we found the pans her dad had used. It was actually fun. We worked hard on the panning but from time to time we just farted around splashing water on one another. We were finding gold, however. Lots of gold. Not the biggest nuggets I'd ever seen but not the smallest either. They were just right. After we accumulated a supply, we hid our stash in the barn where Lori's dad had hidden his stash.

On another note, we changed the name of the creek to Crow's Creek. Mom and Crow would have loved that.

CHAPTER FORTY-ONE

THE VISIT

About three weeks after I had met Marshal Patrick Mountain, he and his two children arrived at our humble abode. 'Humble abode,' where in the hell did I ever hear a saying like that? I must be dreaming lately. Lori ran out of the cabin and right to our new friends. She looked at Rose and said, "Hi, I'm Lori, come with me and I'll show you my room. You'll be staying in my room with me."

Pat said, "Why hello again Lori, did you not see me here? This is my son Bill, he's also here for a visit too."

Lori realized what she had just done, she said, "I'm so sorry. Hello Mr. Mountain and hello to you Bill. Bill, would you like to come along with us, and I'll show you both around."

Bill shook his head yes and followed the girls. I was standing there staring at Pat. My goodness he's a handsome man. At first, I couldn't talk, I was mesmerized by this good-looking man standing in front of me. I finally realized that I was making a fool of myself standing there with my mouth open, so I said, "Welcome Pat, how was the ride out here?"

Pat smiled and replied, "It was worth the ride to see you again. You have on the dress you bought the other day, and you look beautiful in it. But you'd look beautiful in anything you'd wear. I love your homestead. Would you show me around?"

I said, "Follow me. Let's go into the cabin first."

After we went into the cabin, I could hear the two girls talking. Rose said, "You have your own room, wow, that's really nice. I have to share my room with Bill. Can you imagine having to share your room with a boy?"

Lori said, "I never had any brothers or sisters, so I don't know what that would be like. I wouldn't mind sharing my room with you."

Rose had a big smile on her face and said, "I like you; you and I are going to be good friends."

Bill just stood by and listened to all the girl talk and finally walked outside. I told him to walk down to Crow's Creek and look around. I said, "After I show your dad around, we'll all go fishing. We'll have fish for dinner."

I couldn't believe the smile on his face. His face went from disappointment to happiness in just two seconds. He said, "I love to fish. Thanks Annie."

Pat quickly said, "Son, please call her Miss Crow. It's not polite to call an adult by their first names."

I went over to Bill and gave him a hug and said, "You can call me Annie, I'd like that. You see, I never look at myself as an adult. But as my dear mom used to say, 'You can call me anything you want, but just don't call me late for supper.' She was pretty funny, wasn't she?"

We all laughed, and the day was getting better after all the apprehensions were beginning to disappear. We walked to the barn and the guys looked around. Pat commented, "Boy this is really nice, every man I know would give a lot to have a place like this. And Annie, you have an outhouse here. No one I know in the countryside has one of those things."

I laughed, "When I first came to this site, I was just a little girl about ten years old. I never knew anything like an outhouse existed. We always went into the woods or away from our home to relieve ourselves. My adopted father said he dug the hole for the outhouse, but I found out later he didn't do any work around here. He killed the men that did, and he moved in. They were supposed to be his friends. My adopted mother and I found out later he was a thief and a killer. I'd prefer not to talk about him again because he was such a disappointment to me and Mom."

Pat walked over to me and hugged me. It was so wonderful. I said, "Are you going to hug me every time I tell you a sad story? If so be prepared to do lots of hugging in the future."

"Count on it. It was pretty nice for me too. It's been a longtime since I hugged a full-grown woman."

We walked around the grounds and he looked over the gardens and the wood piles. Back in the house I asked the girls if they'd want to go fishing with us. They politely declined my invitation. I did tell them that we were all going to go swimming later on. I just heard moaning coming from both of them.

Bill had gone back to the barn and got the fishing poles that I made for the occasion. They were just tree branches with hook attached to the string. Lori and I had already dug for the worms we'd use for bait. We fished in the little pond at the end of Crow's Creek. I love saying Crow's Creek. This little pond besides being fed by the creek is also spring fed, at least that is what Crow always told me. Even when the creek is running low the pond is always full. Maybe Crow was right. We caught trout, so many trout. They are what we call cutthroat trout. They're called that because they have pink, red or orange marks on their underside that makes the fish look like their throat has been cut. Now, at least that's what I've told.

After catching the fish, we needed to clean them, and my new friend Bill wanted no part of that. Lori was close by when he said he wouldn't be cleaning any fish. She said in a very condescending way, "What are you, a little girl? You cut and clean everything you kill. No exceptions to that rule just ask my mom."

Bill looked my way, and I nodded my head yes and said, "You catch, shoot or trap any type of animal or fish, you clean it, you gut it and we all eat it. Nothing goes to waste."

"Do I have to? I don't want to."

I replied, "You don't want to? If that's the case, you don't eat. Sorry but those are the rules of our homestead, nothing goes to waste. Either you do the work required or you don't eat. That rules goes back to when I was your age. Sorry."

Pat walked up to me and said, "Can I talk to you in private?" We walked a short way away from the kids and he said, "Annie, can we please let him be? I don't push my kids into doing something they don't want to do."

I looked at him and I couldn't believe what I just heard from him. I asked, "You're kidding me, you have to be? You'd let him walk away from doing what we asked him to do? Come on man, that is crazy. You let him get away with that bullshit? Not on my watch. He'll clean those fish just like I'll have to do. We caught them, so we clean them, end of story."

Pat quietly said, "My son lost his mom, and he is still in mourning. Just let it go this one time, please."

I just looked at him and asked, "Didn't you say back in the Gulch that your wife has been dead for over five years? Five years? You think he's still in mourning? After five years? Listen you ass, I lost all my family members twice. Do you think for one minute I had time to mourn for five years? I had to do what my mom used to say, 'shit or get off the pot.' I'm sorry Pat but this is not going to work around here, I think you and your family should pack up and leave."

Pat was clearly upset, he said, "You want us to leave now because my son wouldn't clean some fish? Who do you think you are, his mother?"

"No, I'm not his mother, but if I were, he would not have been crying, moaning and moping around for five fucking long years. It's time for all of you to face reality, she's dead, she's not coming back, so get on with your lives. And if cleaning a few fish is too much for you, I pity you and your future."

Pat walked away and said to Bill and Rose, "We're leaving and we're leaving right now."

Bill said, "Dad, maybe Annie's right. I think I've been acting like a big baby. I know I can get away with anything I want with you and so can Rose. We've talked about it. You give in to anything we want. I like it here. I hate it at home, living in a place where I can't even go outside is no fun. And you're always working and we are always alone. Don't make us leave here, we like it and we both like Lori and Annie. This has been the most fun we've ever had. Annie I'm so sorry, please teach me how to clean the fish. And if we go hunting will you show me how to shoot and how to gut our kill."

Pat was surprised. Maybe surprised wasn't a strong enough word, maybe shocked or embarrassed were better words. He looked at Bill and couldn't say a word. He then looked at me and he looked dumbfounded. He was finally able to say, "I'm so sorry Annie. I'm so embarrassed for the way I acted. You were right. I guess I gave into everything they wanted because I was never home. Working was my way of forgetting my pain. You're correct, it was over five years ago we lost her and it's time for all of us to move on. You are such a strong woman it may have been easier for you, but it hasn't been for us. Please forgive me."

"Pat, I'm not that strong. I got hooked on Laudanum after I was shot, at the time I had lost all my family members including my husband and my two daughters. It was a way to drown my sorrows, but it almost killed me. That's when I realized I had to move on, which I did. You have two nice kids. Lori and I would like you all to stick around but we all have to follow rules. Everyone including Lori and I will follow the rules; it's called being a family."

Bill was the first to speak to me, "Let's clean some fish."

As we walked toward the barn, Pat whispered, "You were shot? Was that the only time?"

I smiled and said, "You don't want to know."

"Yes, I do, I want to know everything about you."

I said, "Let me think. I was shot three times in one episode many years ago. Twice on the day my entire family died. And one more when I had my final run in with the last of the Young boys. So, I think I have six gunshot scars on my body."

"You've got to be kidding me? I heard rumors about you, but I just couldn't believe a woman could have done all the things they said you did. You are truly a legend in these parts. I admire you."

I felt a tug on my sleeve, and it was Lori. She quietly said so no one else could hear, "You said the word fuck. I heard you plain as day. What about out pinky swear?" She smiled and continued, "I'm just kidding you. I say that word all the time when I'm alone." She laughed and ran away. What a kid.

CHAPTER FORTY-TWO

LIFE MOVES ON

The Mountain family stayed with us for a week before Pat said he'd have leave and go back to work. The kids didn't want to leave so they asked him if they could stay for another week. They pleaded with him to let them stay and he agreed to let them as long as Lori and I agreed. I told Pat we'd love to have them stay, as did Lori.

Before Pat left, he and I went for a walk into the woods but very close to the house. He said to me, "I hate leaving you. I just don't know what to do. Annie, I hate my job and I've hated it for a very long time. At first it was the danger; I was always worried some drifter or gunman would shoot me in the back and I'd leave my family with no place to go. Things have gotten better but I still worry. I can't begin to tell you how I feel about you, because I don't want to scare you off. You are the best thing I've had in my life for a very long time. And my kids, they love you and Lori. What am I to do?"

I smiled and said, "You must know I feel the same way about you. I lost my entire family and the good Lord brought me back here to find Lori. I now have a daughter back and I now have you and your kids. Don't you think all the kissing we did this past week means something to me? You are driving me crazy. I don't want to lose you or the kids. I want them to stay with us forever. I know Lori does as well, she told me so. You go back to work and think about it. We have time but I'd like for us to be together. Hurry back in a week, I'll take good care of the kids."

Pat left and we were all very sad. The next week was horrible for me. I missed him so. The kids were great together. They played and did their lessons and chased our dog Ronnie around the yard. At night we locked up the cabin so no one could get in. I read stories to them and we played card games. A real family.

Ten days later Pat rode into the yard in the very early morning. He knocked on the door and woke us all up. He yelled, "Open up I'm finally here. I opened the door and there he stood. He grabbed my hand and moved in for a hug. He then kissed me passionately on my lips and I kissed him right back. I needed him so. We thought that the kids had not seen us kiss before this, but they had. As they were watching us kiss, they all laughed, clapped and Lori said "Yippie, they finally kissed in front of us."

After everyone had settled down a bit and we got dressed in our working clothes, Pat asked me if we could have a talk. He said, "I'm not sure you'll want to hear this, but I quit my job last week. I spent the last few days cleaning up some files for the next guy. Now, I don't know what I'll do to make a living, but I know I'll find something. I hope you're not disappointed in me. I'm not going to take advantage of you, I will find work. Annie, I had to get away from that job. I've been threatened so many times and I know that there are certain gangs still looking for me and wanting to kill me. I just hope you understand why I quit. Also, in this country, when you find someone to love you, you have to tell her right away before she gets away. So, I'm telling you now."

I smiled at him and said, "You quit your job? How in the hell are you going to support us in the lifestyle we're accustomed too? You lazy man." I looked at him and I thought he was going to cry. I said, "I'm kidding! I'm kidding! I wanted you to quit that job. I want you here and I want you here permanently. I never want you to leave. I know you don't think we're rich, but we do have some gold. That place we call Crow's Creek has gold in it. Lori told me about how her dad was the first to find the stuff. We have a bunch of it hidden in the barn. We'll all have to pan for more until it dries up. I do think we'll need to find out if this property is part of the Homestead Act, if so, we'll need to buy it. If not, we'll just stay here until someone claims it. After you get settled, would you take all of us to Billings and we can find out about our property,"

"Yes, we'll leave in two days. I also want you to know I have some money saved. I never spent any money on lodging or food. The towns I worked in took care of all of that. They had to in order to get men to work in law enforcement. As you know it's very dangerous. So, I have about a thousand dollars saved. That should help us out for a while."

I replied, "I don't care if you have any money, I just want you and the kids to be here with us. Another thing, you'll be sleeping with me in my bedroom. I don't know how you'll explain that to the kids but that will be your job, not mine. We could have a marriage ceremony, how about that? Is it too early for that?"

"No, it's not too early, let's do it today."

Lori wanted all of us to dress up for the wedding. We all gathered in the yard and Lori was the official. She was a no-nonsense type of girl, she wanted everyone to be serious. She asked us if we prepared our vows and we both said we had. We read our vows to one another and the final part of the marriage ceremony was a pinky swear. Lori took that part very seriously since that is what I told her we did in my first marriage. After the marriage vows were said and the pinky swear was completed, it was off to the cabin for lunch. After lunch we all got into our work clothes and headed for Crow's Creek, to pan for gold.

Having a family again was so nice and having a man I loved in my life again was so special. After we had accumulated a few nuggets from our Creek we all headed up to the house. The kids sat on the floor and played card games, while Pat and I just stared at each other. We could hardly wait for bedtime. Around ten o'clock Pat declared it was bedtime. Everyone went to their appointed bed, including Pat and me. He whispered, "I don't know if I can be really quiet, it's been a very long time."

I smiled at him and said, "I'll try and be quiet for the first five times, but after that look out."

He whispered back, "The first five times? Who do you think you married, a god? I'll be lucky with two times, maybe three with the appropriate amount of rest."

I laughingly said, "Appropriate amount of rest? What's that a week or so?" I then began to tickle him, and we began our fun. It did last the appropriate amount of time, we lasted for three sessions. Afterwards, Pat proclaimed. "That was wonderful, I only wish I could go three more times."

I smiled and said, "Just wait until tomorrow, I expect at least four times since we have all day."

Pat quickly replied, "Oh, I forgot to tell you, we're going to Billings tomorrow. I'm thinking only twice tomorrow." We laughed, cuddled and finally feel asleep. I have to admit it was the best I've slept in a very long while. Pat said the same thing. Life is nice.

CHAPTER FORTY-THREE

BILLINGS

We packed up and headed for Billings Montana. We put the kids in the wagon with Bill in charge of the team. Pat and I rode our horses. I changed my dress from a bit formal for me, to very casual. You know, dungarees, plain blue shirt, boots and my six-gun in my holster hanging around my waist. My hair was in my normal braided ponytail, my grizz claw necklace around my neck and I felt really good. Pat was dressed very causal too and he also wore his six-gun on his hip.

It took longer than we thought it would. We had to sleep outside for the first time in quite a while and the kids loved it. Pat's kids had been cooped up in a house for a couple of years so this was a big treat.

On the second day we arrived in Billings and it was booming. The trains had finally gotten to Billings and there was new construction everywhere. I'd never seen such activity. There were still men toting guns and there were many saloons that advertised whores. When I say many saloons, I couldn't begin to count all of them.

Pat said knew someone in the government office building where we could get information on the Homestead Act. Under that Act, the government would offer government land to an applicant so they could acquire ownership. The Act, which was made into law in 1862, offered 160 acres to any US citizen that would farm the land. We knew we'd qualify; it was just a matter of finding out if our property could be homesteaded and paying whatever the cost would be.

Pat introduced me to his friend Fred Hopkins at the land office and we explained where our land was. He was able to find it on a map mostly because of Crow's Creek and the pond and also the woods behind the house. Fred said that no one had laid claim to that property. But since so much of the property was made up of just trees, he offered an alternative. There was a new act called The Timber Culture Act of 1873, that granted ownership to people who were required to plant trees on their existing homestead. Since we had been living on that property for years, we would qualify. The cost was only $1.25 per acre for 320 acres, but we were required to plant trees on at least forty acres. The nice part was that we already had more than forty acres of trees. Since we had been living on over a hundred acres already, we were required to pay for only 220 acres. The cost was $275, which we had carried with us in gold nuggets. Fred accepted our gold as payment and told us we were lucky. Property around us in that area was getting to be in big demand. With the taming of Settlers Gulch, it had become an area where families wanted to settle.

We walked out of the land office with big smiles on our faces. In a few days we'd be required to return to Billings and collect our deed. Things were looking up, until we visited the Marshal's Office. Pat wanted to see his old friends and introduce me to them. He thought it would be best to leave the kids in the store, they were having so much fun.

We walked down the street from the land office and walked into the Marshal's office. We were greeted there by Lance Pittman, who helped run the office and was the third in command for the whole district, including Settlers Gulch.

Pat introduced me as Annie his wife. Lance asked, "Annie, what is your maiden name?"

I replied with a smile, "Why, it was first O'Grady and then I was adopted by a man named Crow, so I changed it to Crow. And Crow it has been since I was a little girl."

Lance smiled right back at me and said, "I thought it was you. Not too many women named Annie around here and not many tote a six-shooter either. You likely don't know this, but you are a wanted woman. I've been looking for you for a couple of years now. Seems you killed a defenseless man in Coulson some time back and you ran away. His brother came to us sometime later and asked that we find you and have you prosecuted. We also heard other rumors about you killing other miners and drifters. They say you kill at random, just for the sport of it. Miss Crow, would that be true?"

I stared at him and didn't answer. He finally said, "Did you hear me, is what I said correct?"

I replied, "No, that is not correct. I've never killed anyone that didn't deserve killing. If you think I did, prove it."

"Well, that will be a problem. Your accuser is no longer around these parts, maybe you killed him too. I'm going to keep you here until I can determine if you are the person I'm looking for."

I was ready to draw my six-gun when Pat said, "Lance, you check it out, but I don't think you'll find anyone that will want to attest to Annie killing anyone. Can you please release her to me, and I guarantee that I'll bring her back if and when you might want to interrogate her again?"

Lance appeared to be in deep thought, and finally said, "I trust you Pat, but I'm not sure I trust her. She has a bad reputation around here."

I interrupted the both of them, I said, "How long have you been in this part of the country Lance? I'm guessing you've been here for a very short time. You have no idea what it was like being a woman around here. Women were accosted, beaten, raped and killed by the men I killed. Yes, I said the men I killed. I always killed in self-defense.

In case you didn't hear me, always self-defense! I was accosted every time I entered a town by assholes like the ones you're talking about. That asshole wanted me for sex. But not for only him, but for all his friends. Of course, I refused, and he and his friends were going to take me by force. Now, I gave him a chance, but he grabbed my gun by the barrel and moved it way from his throat. I then took out my Bowie knife and I shoved it into his balls. I walked away with him crying like a baby. I didn't know if he died or not. Do you know why? Because it was him or me and I just didn't give a shit. If you want to try and take me and put me in jail, you'll die trying. I do not stand for bad behavior in a man, I just won't. And you Lance, are exhibiting bad behavior. You just assume because a man says I killed his brother that is a clear case of murder, well it's not. I'm leaving here now with my family, if you try and stop me, you'll see me in action, and I don't miss. Your case against me is just hearsay, nothing more nothing less."

Lance stood in deep thought, he said," Are you threatening me? I'm a peace officer and that is against the law."

I replied, "Are you threatening me? That is also against the law. But if you think you can outdraw me, go for it."

Pat stepped in and said, "This type of back and forth will get us nowhere. No one is going to draw down on the other person. Lance you are being unreasonable, Annie is right. Your accusations are baseless, and you know it. If you check around these parts, you'll find out Annie took down the Young brothers. Do you think that was not justified? They killed her entire family and left her for dead. When they found out she was alive, they came after her again. There was no law and order at the time, when she was forced to kill them. Do you really think a judge will want to try a woman that is a legend in Montana? I think not. Now if you continue this bullshit with my wife, I'll gladly go over your head."

Lance was going to begin to refute Pat, but his colleague in the other room stepped out and said, "Howdy Pat. And Annie, I've always wanted to meet you. I'm Roy Peters. Pat is correct, you are a legend around this part of Montana, and I think in many other areas of our territory too. You'll have to forgive my associate Lance here; he does not know about your heroics. Lance, this woman was the law and order around here before we were hired. She singlehandedly got rid of the worst gang ever around here, the Young brothers. I think you owe her an apology; your comments are clearly baseless."

Lance was upset to say the least, he held back his temper and quietly said, "I don't think I'm wrong. No sir, I don't! We can't just let killers walk away free. No sir!"

"Lance, I've killed eight men over the years, all bad men. Do I deserve to go to jail? No, because I wear a badge. So, if we would have given Annie here a badge, would it have been alright for her to kill those outlaws? Yes, it would have been. If you persist in this bad behavior as Anne calls it, I will be forced to remove you from your post and send you farther west. You know, farther west is where they're killing lawmen. Understand? Do you understand?"

Lance replied, "Screw you Roy. If you let her go, I'll go over your head. I won't tolerate bad behavior in my boss. I'll quit! And you Miss Annie; the killer of men, women and children. I won't allow you to continue this charade, I'll make sure the higher ups around here know I found you and this so-called Director, will lose his job and maybe go to jail himself. Watch out for me, I'll be coming for you."

Roy quietly said, "Lance please come with me." Lance reluctantly followed Roy into to an office and we could hear everything that was being said. Roy began, "I've been to Washington DC to visit our home office there. I spoke to our Director of National Security a Mr. John Bowden. John asked me about Annie Crow when I was there. He had heard rumors about her feats in dealing with outlaws. He asked me how we could honor her legacy. He thought she was dead, as all of us did. I just told him that maybe we could get a writer to tell her story. What you don't know, is that there is an author named Spencer Wilmot on his way out here right now to write the story about her life. Now, at the time I didn't realize Annie had survived the murder of her family. So, I hope you realize Washington does not want Annie's reputation to be tarnished by some low-ranking person in Billings Montana. If you want to leave the marshal's service be my guest. If you want to stay, you'll do as we say. Annie Crow is untouchable, and she is a hero to all of us. You will respect her."

Lance said, "I'm sorry boss, I guess I just got carried away. I'll apologize to her immediately."

Lance walked out and extended his hand to me to shake. I said, "Get away from me. I don't ever want to see you again. If you try and make small talk with me you better go for your gun. I won't tolerate bad behavior in a man, and you have shown nothing but bad behavior. If you ever dare come close to me or my family, I'll shoot you down."

Lance hightailed it out of that office as soon as I told him I may shoot him, which I'd never do. After Lance had left the office, Roy asked, "Annie, would you mind talking to a writer from Washington about your life? I mean it would be a book about your life. We think it would make a great story and would also help us recruit lawmen to come farther west. What do you think? Would you meet with Mr. Wilmot?"

I replied, "Sure, why not? If he wants to talk to me, however, he'll have to come out to our homestead, I'm not coming back here ever again. Pat will be back in a few days to pick up the deed to our property, he can follow him to out to our home. But I will tell you one thing in advance, you make sure he tells the whole truth and nothing but the truth. I don't want people to think I'm a senseless killer. And I want to read the story before it is printed."

CHAPTER FORTY-FOUR

EPILOGUE

After I reread the contents of this book for about the millionth time, I always say I like it and it's a very truthful story of my life. I realize now it is 1905 and I think I am over 50 years old. My God, 50 years old. No wonder Patrick only wants to have sex five times a week instead of every day like we used to. Needless to say, I am a very happy woman.

Pat and I had a daughter fifteen years ago and we named her after my friend, Manda. All of our kids are doing well. I home schooled them until they got to be twelve years old. They then attended school in the Gulch, and they stayed at my friends Mike and Carol Gorman's house three days a week until summertime. Mike as you might recall is the owner of Gorman's General Store in the Gulch and they have become our family's best friends.

Our children have all been good kids and we love them so. After losing my family twice, I realize God has blessed me. Who gets a second chance or a third chance at having a family? Lori and Rose are married to men they met in the Gulch and both have one child, both girls. Lori's daughter carries my name of Annie Crow and Rose's daughter is named Sue after my mom. Bill is single and is working for the US Marshal's office in Billings. He has a girlfriend named Kim and they are in love. Manda is fifteen going on thirty, just like my little Addie-Lou always was. Pat has been the best husband a woman with my background could have ever expected to have gotten. We love each other so much. Life has been troublesome but also very good and rewarding for me.

This book is my life story. It took a long time to be written, since the original author Mr. Wilmot died one year after our time together. I had nothing to do with his death, please believe me. Jim Pierce another author, and Wilmot's son-in-law, asked if he could finish my story after reading what Mr. Wilmot had begun writing. He told me he was intrigued with the story of my life and was hopeful readers would feel the same way. It was finally completed and published ten years later and has been very successful. I hope you enjoyed reading about my life and the old west and all the hardships we endured trying to tame it. It was a rough and tumble life, but I wouldn't change any of it.

Sincerely,

Annie Crow

Annie Crow

ACKNOWLEDGEMENTS

I'd like to acknowledge all my friends and relatives that encouraged me, supported me and read all my past books, no matter how good or bad they were. Their names are as follows;

My wife LaVonne Mountain, my sons, Patrick Mountain, Mark Mountain and Scott Mountain. Also, my daughter-in-law Emilia Mountain and my grandson William Mountain. My sister, Kate Mountain Dass and her daughter Jill Martin and her husband Steve. My friends, Larry Podobinski, Mike and Carol Gorman, Jerry Guptil, Ted Boran, Ron Naslund, Roger Young, Jack Daugherty, Harry Daly, Hartley Smith, Jim and Sandy Anderson, Scott Hutton, Peter Schenk, Hunter Schenk and Larry Sondrall. I know that I missed a few names but please forgive me, I'm getting old.

ABOUT THE AUTHOR

I was born and raised in south Minneapolis. I worked in the securities business for over forty years.

After a trip to my family's hometown of Killeagh, Ireland, I became interested in my genealogy. I researched my family background and made the decision that it would be a good fictional book. The first book in the trilogy is, **The Saga of the Brothers Mountain.** The second book was titled **William,** followed by **WJ American Hero.**

After completing the trilogy of the Mountain family, I continued to write several other fictional books. The titles of the other books are; **Padraig Murphy, Semper Fi, The Foster Lake Love Affair**, **Will Cobb, The One-Armed Gunslinger, Father Mitchell Collins, The Hunt for Kevin Hart, and last but not least, The Legend of Annie Crow.**

Made in the USA
Monee, IL
19 July 2021

73243308R00125